Ghosted

Emma Kathryn

GenZ
The Future of Publishing

For ma wee maw, Fiona, who read my first ever book to me.
(But who doesn't like scary stories. Sorry, Mum!)

This book contains a scene of suicide and discussions on the topic.

Introduction

Him

I wake with a start and rattle the objects I am trapped in this bloody box with. Four cardboard walls crush me, its poorly taped-down flaps mocking me. Sometimes, I think that I see light coming through the thin packing tape. I groan and push at the edges of my prison. I've been waiting for someone to come along and wake me for fifteen years, and now, here it is.

If my lungs still worked, I'd be choking on the dust I've just shifted. Instead, the particles pass through me, escaping from a tear in the corner of the box. They laugh at me as they drift away while I'm still stuck.

Noise fills the house for the first time in years. Boxes thump, furniture is drilled together, and harsh words are thrown around from time to time. I curl inside my space as much as I can and listen carefully. Somebody is moving in. I had given up hope that anybody would actually want to live in this bloody house again and it's been so very lonely.

Introduction

Two female voices ring out. Both are frustrated, but one speaks words edged with anger. The anger calls to me: it sounds like things I would've screamed at my bloody parents. It wakes something inside me.

I uncoil further and press my hand to the attic floor. A bedroom door slams—my bedroom. She has claimed my bedroom as hers. Something in me wriggles with excitement. This is it. I'm getting out of here.

My prison sits directly above where she places her bed: I can tell from all the noise. More boxes crash and bang until eventually, she flops down on the bed. I hear the mattress springs sighing along with her. She begins to cry loudly.

My cheek lies along the floor, directly above her head. I imagine lying down with her and wrapping her in my cold, dead arms. Her pain sings, and I strain to hear it. She's so sad. I was just as sad in that bedroom once. Nobody cared when I cried.

I will save her. I will stop her crying and bring her to my side. I've been so lonesome up here, abandoned and friendless. But now, there's hope—and she's lying in my bedroom.

From somewhere in the house, I hear her mother call out to her.

"Flora," she calls.

Flora. Her name is Flora. And I can't wait to see her face.

Chapter One

Flora

Blairness High School glared down at me with judgement. Here was the wild Glaswegian girl that was going to ruin your nice, quiet Highland town. I looked up at the "Welcome!" sign, and sighed heavily as I braced myself for my first day in a new school. My uniform had that horrible, new crisp feeling, and the blazer kept making the back of my neck itch. This was going to be terrible.

After the excruciating visit to the school office, a disapproving office lady looked me up and down. Eventually, she offered to give me the tour and then escort me to my first class: English. I could cope with that. The corridors seemed small as we walked to the languages department, like a model of a high school rather than the giant aircraft hangar of a building that I'd spent my last four years in.

Emma Kathryn

My tour took all of five minutes. Cafeteria over there, library down that hall, lockers there. Now get to class.

Riveting stuff.

The classroom I was dumped at was even worse. The office woman swung the door open and announced, "New girl, Mrs Hill. This is Flora James."

I groaned as I was pushed in front of the class and the office lady vanished. So, this is what being thrown in at the deep end actually felt like. Two people near the back of the room sniggered. I glanced awkwardly at Mrs Hill, a greying woman in her fifties who was in no hurry to get me in a seat. I took a deep breath in and surveyed the twenty-four faces pointed in my direction. None of them seemed very defined—they were all just student-shaped blobs right now—and I had no names to attach to them. All of them knew *my* name though. They all knew I was Flora, that I was shorter than the average teenager, and that my wild black hair was entirely untameable. Awkwardly, I tried to push my mad mane of black back away from my face, as if that would help somehow.

"Flora," Mrs Hill announced. "What a lovely name."

"Thanks," I grunted, trying not to look at the sea of faces again. My accent sounded really rough next to hers.

"Quiet one, eh?" she laughed, still making no attempt to get me to a desk quickly. "Let's get you some books."

I waited patiently, trying to ignore the whispers.

She continued, "You must be missing Glasgow! Coming all the way up here!"

Oh God, no. She was going to ask me questions.

"Yeah," I said, as quietly as I could. "It was a bit of a trek."

Mrs Hill burst out laughing, and all the heads in the class lifted. "Very funny, dear."

A couple of people laughed, but I couldn't work out if that was in my favour or not. I just smiled, nodded and silently thanked God, Buddha, and Elvis when she eventually pointed me in the direction of a seat.

More people giggled. I half-hoped they were laughing at her rather than at me, but it seemed unlikely. Heat rose from my chin and travelled to the tips of my ears. I wanted to go home —real home, not this makeshift home.

Opening up my new textbook, I found the assigned reading analysis questions. Luckily, English was one of my better subjects, and I could try to focus on the work rather than the humiliation I was facing as a weird new kid in a tiny northern school. My little flurry of fear and panic and rage was beginning to dissipate with each passing reading question. Focusing on metaphors and sound techniques momentarily helped me forget about the pack of wolves surrounding me.

Before I lost myself in the words, I thought I imagined voices whispering about me. I heard them picking on my mad hair and my strong Glaswegian accent, which made me sound a lot rougher than these Highland folk.

A bit of folded paper landed on my desk. A hiss from diagonally behind me heralded its arrival. I turned around to see a preppy boy with the most perfect hair I'd ever seen on a human being. In fact, he didn't even look human; he looked like a Sim. I'm talking a pre-loaded Sim that comes with the game, not any of the haphazard hobos I end up designing.

Emma Kathryn

He gestured for me to read the note. Glancing at his desk, it didn't look like he'd actually attempted any work. Instead, his phone was sticking out from under the textbook's open cover. I must have stared at him with a look of confusion for a little too long because when he repeated the gesture, he coupled it with some fresh disdain. I unfolded the note and read:

YOU LIVE AT 1 MOCKINGBIRD LANE

I instantly formed a dislike for this person. The right thing to do here would have been to ignore the note. Unfortunately, this had not been a good day for me. I was still glowing crimson from my first round of humiliation after standing at a desk for ages and this seemed to further fuel my stupidity. Somewhat foolishly, I wrote back:

LOCATION SERVICES HAVE BEEN DISABLED FOR THIS USER.

I passed it over as quickly as I could. This kind of behaviour was probably adding to the everyone-thinks-I'm-loopy vibe I was getting from the class. A small snort came from his desk. Mrs Hill didn't look up. Apparently, she didn't bother with note-passers in her class. The note was swiftly returned with a response:

I KNOW YOU DO

MY MUM WAS THE ESTATE AGENT

Surely this was a breach of data protection laws or estate agent-client privilege. Did this so-called professional just go home and sit at the dining table and say, "Guess who's coming to town, family? A miserable divorcee and her even more miserable teenage daughter!" I threw a disgusted face his way, and he smirked with all-too-perfect teeth. They were the kind of teeth that come from tooth whitener and night-time retainers. God forbid his teeth have any kind of character. I scrawled an angry response:

THIS IS BEYOND CREEPY. WHAT ARE YOU TRYING TO SAY, STALKER BOY?

Another snort escaped him, and I watched as he elbowed his friend at the desk next to his. The friend looked over, pulling out a rather indiscreetly hidden earbud (the old cable-up-the-shirt-and-leaning-your-head-towards-your-shoulder trick). My note was shared. Without my permission, too. Another data protection breach—like mother, like son. The friend laughed aloud. Mrs Hill cleared her throat but made no attempt to investigate. Another note was scribbled and thrown my way. This time there were two sets of eyes judging me.

YOU LIVE IN A MURDER HOUSE

A DUDE DIED IN THERE

. . .

At that point, I decided to stop writing back to the pretty boy at least. His use of the word "dude" without a hint of irony broke me. Also, you know, the "murder house" bit—mostly the "Murder House" bit, actually. I took out my phone and took a picture of the note, WhatsApping it to my three best friends back home: Lucy, Suzie, and Scott. I added the caption: "*Apparently, I live in the* Addams Family *mansion now.*" I nearly sent it to Dani, my ex, out of habit, but thought better of it.

In spite of her ignoring the note-swapping session, Mrs Hill decided that she couldn't ignore a phone in class, and *my phone* was confiscated. Not the idiot and his friend who had been throwing notes at me. Oh no, she didn't take theirs.

At the end of the lesson, when I tried to get my phone back, she instead decided to lecture me on the difficulties of divorce since she had read my pastoral care notes. More crimson bloomed in my face. Surely, she wasn't meant to tell me this?!

I nodded and uh-huh-ed at her until she shut up long enough for me to take my leave. I hated this school, I hated this class, I hated this teacher.

Someone. Sack. Her. Now.

The rest of the day was a blur of meeting teachers, getting homework, dodging the chaos of the cafeteria, getting more homework, awkward introductions, and getting even more homework. By the time the final bell rang, I was bloody exhausted.

The walk home was forty minutes in countryside drizzle. Leaving school, I had to travel through the village with my head down. Other students filed past me in twos and threes, laughing and joking. A bunch of boys bounded by, wrestling one another. One shoved another into me. They all laughed, and one muttered something that sounded a little like sorry. I stumbled backwards and tried to keep out of their way. They weren't sorry.

A loud clatter behind me sent me jumping but as I turned around, I discovered a boy on a skateboard. A *skateboard,* on this side of the millennium. His dark, floppy hair was familiar, and I recognised him as one of the student-shaped-blobs in my English class, but not the one who had thrown me notes about knowing where I live. I must have stared a little too long but, unlike the note-thrower, the Skater just gave me a nod as he slid by me. I nodded back awkwardly and watched him weave through the crowd to cross the road.

He met up with a girl dressed entirely in black. She had a flair for the Winona Ryder look, circa 1988. Something was muttered, and then the girl dropped her jaw in disbelief. She scanned the small crowd of students until she found me. A frantic wave went up in my general direction. I dropped my eyes and turned away as quickly as I could. I did not need any more of this today. I just wanted to get back to that stupid house and demand to Mum that we move back home immediately. Maybe this daft excursion had made her forgive Dad long enough for us to go back home. Maybe?

To avoid more stares and unsolicited waving incidents, I busied myself with looking at my phone. My picture message had been read by none of my friends back home. Maybe they just hadn't seen it yet. I sent a sassy message about skateboards. They'd definitely have to respond by the time I got to the house, right?

I started my walk through the sleepy town of Blairness, which we had given up the bright lights of Glasgow for. It was maybe about an hour's drive from the city of Inverness, somewhere that might have felt a little more like home than this tiny place. I sighed as I went for a trip through somewhere that looked like a "Visit Scotland" advert. I walked past shops and bakers and homes and more cobblestone streets than anyone would struggle to walk on as I made my way back to the place Mum had insisted on calling home.

After fifteen minutes through town, I was in the thick of the countryside. A tiny path on the side of the road paved my way, and I had to practically press up against a little stone wall every time a car passed. I was caught short by at least two cars going through puddles. By the time I reached the dirt road that led up to the house, I was soaked. My umbrella was doing no good, and I had to give up on it as I passed the wide lake that lay between the main road and my stupid new house.

Some ducks and a couple of angry geese waggled their pointed bums and flapped their wings against the inclement weather. They were having a way better time than me. Some little ducklings were making noises out on the tiny island in the middle of the lake, but I couldn't see them through the thick weeds and tall grass that grew there. High-pitched quacks welcomed me home. Trudging through the muddy road, I pledged to remember to wear my welly boots to school tomorrow and ditch them in my brand-new locker before class started.

The house rose in the distance. It was all height and points, like a skeletal hand reaching up to grasp at something dangling from the clouds but never quite reaching it. Windows sat in overly elaborate frames, and I desperately wished we had the money to get them replaced with regular-looking rather than fear-inducing windows. Wildflowers and weeds crawled up the porch steps as if leading the way to the front door. I looked up and tried to work out which rooms I could see from here. My room was at the back of the house, but you could see Mum's bedroom window and a small box room from the front. A large dirty smudge was smeared across the box room window, like someone had pressed some kind of greasy creature up against the glass before it scrambled loose and escaped to dirty up the rest of the house.

It was basically the house from the *Amityville Horror*.

When I got inside, I found my mother in what had once been described as a dining room, rearranging books while polishing off a glass of wine. The boxes with the rest of the glasses had not been unpacked yet but, rest assured, one wine glass had been reclaimed. Her dark hair was tied up, away from her face, and her glasses were slipping towards the edge of her nose. She hid her slim figure under a pair of dungarees and a t-shirt with light pink stripes. She was clearly still in mucking-out-the-new-house mode, judging by her clothes.

"How was your day, Sweetie?" Mum asked as she found a place on the shelf for Helen Fielding. She must have just put the bookcases up today. I could bet that pocket on the front of her dungarees was hiding spare nails and screws from today's DIY project. She'd actually done a pretty good job. Two walls were now covered with bookcases, and she'd filled about half of them with books so far.

I sighed. "You know that bit in *Mean Girls* where Lindsay Lohan isn't a bitch yet and has to eat lunch in the toilet because everyone thinks she's a home-schooled freak? That."

Mum looked up, empty wine glass in hand. "I've never seen *Mean Girls*," she said, as casually as one might say *"Oh, I've never been to Mars."*

"You're a disgrace of a human being," I told her. I started towards the huge wooden stairs before I remembered my note session with the note-boy and doubled back on myself. "By the way, thanks for buying a murder house, Mum."

"What are you on about?" Mum asked, her voice filled with irritation.

"Well, because this is the tiniest town in all of Scotland, the estate agent's son is in my English class. He said someone was murdered in this house. Super murdered."

Mum dismissed me with a wave of the hand. "No one was murdered, Flora. Don't be so melodramatic. But yes, I did know that there had been some kind of family tragedy here."

My eyes widened with disbelief, and my jaw dropped. "Don't be melodramatic? Someone died in this house! I could get attacked by a zombie at any time! And I bet 'family tragedy' is estate-agent-chat for 'murder house'."

Scooping up her glass, Mum rolled her eyes and breezed right by me towards the kitchen. I followed swiftly to ensure that she knew this conversation was far from over.

"Family tragedy means that someone died here, yes," Mum answered as we played follow-the-leader through the hallway. "The house lay empty for a few years, and then someone must have decided it was time to get rid of it. How

10

do you think we ended up getting it so cheap, Flora? We're not made of money."

"So that's why we moved to the arse-end of nowhere?" I snapped, but I was cut off when the kitchen door opened, and an amazing smell smacked me in the face. "Oh my God, what is that smell?" I said as I inhaled a delicious aroma. I abandoned my last angry thought for this newer, tastier one.

Mum started to busy herself around the kitchen. "First of all: language," she reprimanded me. "Second: I made a Thai green curry for dinner."

The kitchen was the definition of the word "rustic". It was going to need a lot of work, but Mum seemed to take this on with gusto. I knew that she'd seen the large island in the middle of the room and the Belfast sink under the window and fallen in love. She knew she'd get to the bits that needed fixing eventually. Glancing over at the cooker, I could see a simmering pan. My mother, it seemed, was indeed telling the truth. She had cooked.

My eyebrows displayed my surprise. "What?" I asked. "No frozen pizza or oven chips?"

Mum refilled her wine glass.

"Nope. I figured that the first day of a new school deserved a half-decent meal. It's made from scratch, so it's only got the veggies you like in it. With plenty of extra spicy crackers, too. And since I'm such an uncultured swine, we can eat it in the living room, and you can introduce me to *Mean Girls*."

It was difficult for me to hide how happy this made me. I couldn't let her think she'd gotten away with it, though. She did divorce Dad, run away from Glasgow, and buy a house where someone was probably brutally butchered and other such horrors.

"Don't think this means I'm forgiving you for this being a scary murder house," I faux-grumbled.

"Yeah, yeah," Mum said. "Now go get ready for dinner. And bring the DVD down. I'm not attempting to search through Netflix for it."

Last time we tried to watch the latest episode of *RuPaul's Drag Race* on Netflix, Mum cried the minute the Netflix *buh-bummmm* sound played and threatened to cancel the account. I managed to calm her down with a glass of wine and reminded her that they'd just added all of *Grey's Anatomy,* so she couldn't possibly cancel now.

See, we weren't the only ones to escape Glasgow. Part of what had prompted the divorce was Dad getting a shiny new job in London producing a TV show for Netflix. Unfortunately, divorce isn't good for a romance writer, which meant that Mum had to sell our house. So here we are, moved into a decrepit shack in the middle of nowhere, where Mum cries at the Netflix logo and doesn't write anything.

This is the madness I had to live with.

Mum's curry was pretty good. There was way too much of it; sometimes she forgets about Dad not being here and cooks as if there are still three people in the house, even though he was barely ever home in the first place. To compensate, I managed a second helping. We watched *Mean Girls,* and Mum laughed all the way through. There's something really satisfying about sharing something you like with someone else and having them like it too.

We'd eaten and watched in the living room. There was still a lot to be done in there, but Mum had obviously fallen in love with the old fireplace and hearth. It was very much her jam. She loved anything that looked a bit vintage.

During the film, I sent GIFs of my favourite bits to my friends' group chat. They didn't message back, just like they hadn't messaged back earlier. I wondered if they had muted me. I sent Lucy a message separately, asking how things were going. I checked my phone at least five times as I washed off my make-up, brushed my teeth, and put on my PJs. No response. Not even two blue ticks on WhatsApp.

I retreated to my room. It really didn't feel like my room yet. The walls were a dull off-white, and apart from holding my bed, desk, and computer, it could have been anyone's room. It sure as hell wasn't the beautiful purple room I'd put together back in Glasgow.

Before going to sleep, I did my usual rounds on the internet to see how Dad's TV show was coming along. I thought Dad's new show would have been a great thing. For one, it was an adaptation of my favourite book series of all time: the *Archival Cycle*. And two, I thought since Mum wasn't writing so much, Dad landing a fancier job would make sense. Apparently not.

I hit up Twitter, IMDB, and at least three different pop culture sites. There were new set photos of Martin Freeman and Thandiwe Newton in fantasy make-up and costumes, running in front of green screens, but no sign of Dad. He wouldn't ever have been in set photos anyway. This I knew well, which made it even stupider for me to scour the images in as much detail as I had.

I devolved into an even bigger idiot and thumbed my way through Dani's Instagram. My ex stared back at me from post-gym pictures in front of a bathroom mirror, group selfies, and Boomerangs of dancing with people I used to dance with. Every picture with me in it had been deleted.

I went to bed defeated, undoing all of the good work Mum had done with *Mean Girls* and the curry.

Him

She cries when she goes to bed. It's the only sound I can hear, and it fills my little box of pain. I don't know why she's crying until she makes a frantic phone call in the middle of the night.

"Lucy, what's going on?" She is trying to sound calm but it's not working. There's a tremor in her voice that reveals her weakness right now. She shouldn't be making this call and she knows it. "It's just that nobody's answering my messages..."

She's cut off by the person on the other line, and I have no idea what's being said. Frustration lingers in my mouth. I want to yell out to her.

Curling in on myself, I try to find the best way to listen in. I'm starting to get angry for her. This box was bad enough for fifteen years of loneliness, but now that something is finally happening, it's keeping me from getting involved. I want to know what's happening.

She continues, "Yeah, but it's not my fault we moved. You guys can visit and I'm sure I can come back to Glasgow from time to time... Oh my God, Luce, the train is totally not that long. It's not... It's not!"

Her desperation verges on delicious. I want to tell her she's embarrassing herself. I want to reach out and take the phone and tell this bitch Lucy to fuck off. I want to hold her afterwards and tell her she doesn't need these people; she just needs me. I'm the only one she'll ever need.

"So that's it?" The tremor in her voice is about to become uncontrollable. "Friendship over? I'm shunned because I moved across the country? Against my will, I'd like to add."

Another silence blooms from the bedroom, floating through the ceiling and laughing at my ignorance. This is excruciating. I wish I was in the room with her. It is my room after all. She's just borrowing it until I can get out of this bloody prison. I pick at the bottom of the box impatiently. Or I try to—nothing I ever do makes any impact on my cardboard confinement.

"Hold on," she interrupts, suddenly swelling with anger rather than fear. "What do you mean, 'Dani and I'? What has Dani got to do with this?"

For a second, the tinny voice of the speakerphone chimes in, but it's far too low for me to pick anything out. Why has she put her on speaker? A girl's voice drones on, and I can't pick anything out at all. This is a goddam nightmare. I want to punch my way out of this box and go down there.

"Stop," she orders the speakerphone. "Tell me this is not a picture of you together on your Instagram."

"You left!" I hear the person on the other end of the line scream through the speakerphone.

Emma Kathryn

She hangs up abruptly, and I spend the rest of the night listening to her cry. She sounds so incredibly lonely.

Like me.

I think if we could talk, we'd understand each other's pain. She'd get me. I know she would. I've been waiting a long time for someone to take away my loneliness. And I think she'll be the one to do it.

I want to kiss her face and taste the tears. I think they'd be delicious.

Chapter Two

Flora

I knew that it was probably an angry phone call with Lucy that kept me up all night, but I couldn't help but feel that it was the house.

Once I had hung up on Lucy, who thought that moving house means you don't ever have to think about the person who moved again, I spent a lot of time studying the room while trying to pretend that my heart wasn't hurting as much as my puffy eyes did. I stared around the room trying to make out familiar shapes in the dark. Boxes were the easiest to spot, and maybe the most comforting too. My desk was also a relief.

However, in the corner of the room, in front of a door that led to a pretty spacious cupboard, was what looked like a person crouching.

My heart leapt into my throat, and I scrambled into a sitting position, yanking my duvet upwards and sending pillows flying. The figure remained still, seemingly unperturbed by my commotion. I kept my bloodshot eyes trained on the shape and blindly felt around the bedside table for my phone. Breathing heavily, I convinced myself that if I looked away, then surely when I looked back it would be standing over me. Visions of a shadowy figure strangling me to death plagued my mind.

At last, I grabbed my phone. With trembling fingers, I turned on my torch function and pointed it aggressively at the invading shape. A bright cone of light illuminated where my school blazer hung from the handle of the cupboard door.

The moment I saw it, I felt completely ridiculous. The memory of hanging it there came back to me.

I sighed and slid back down in bed. I hated Lucy even more now. What a cow. I also hated her because now I needed to pee, which meant I needed to get out of bed and wander the goddam house in the middle of the night.

It is worth making clear that I did not get to see the house prior to moving in. Mum clearly walked in and said, "*Oh yes, this has ample book storing space for very little cash – I'll take it.*" As a non-divorced person, I know that I shouldn't judge her in this heartbroken state (which she keeps refusing to write about or even acknowledge—save for any of the time she spends crying at the logos on streaming services). But, on the other hand, she'd just moved us into a murder house and slapped the name 'Home' onto it like some kind of improvised plaster.

The house's two floors were occupied by two bedrooms, a tiny box room, a toilet, lounge, kitchen, and dining room. The dining room had been turned into a library, because of course it had—it couldn't have been an actual dining room for this family. It instead had to be used for extra book room. Nothing else had much semblance of living space yet. Everything else was still boxes and bin bags.

I had tried to transform my assigned room into something that resembled me, but it was hard to motivate myself when my last bedroom had been sixteen years in the making. My last bedroom had been gorgeous. It had a feature wall with flocked purple wallpaper, so swish that it was ridiculous.

Unable to ignore the pain in my bladder, I climbed out of bed and escaped my ugly bedroom. Without worrying about waking Mum up, I turned on every light I passed on the way to the toilet. While there, I discovered that the tap over the ancient bath was dripping. I tightened it. The dripping stopped.

I returned to my crappy new room and got back into bed, righting my pillows and fixing my duvet. Once lying down, I stared up at the ceiling. A sound irritated my ears, nagging at my mind and keeping me awake a little longer.

The tap was dripping. It was back already.

I hate this house.

Sticking in my headphones, I did my best to force myself to sleep to the tune of Florence and the Machine. Even though I was sure that it was percussion in the music, I was so sure that I could hear the continuing drip over the sounds of Florence's song, "Blinding".

. . .

Emma Kathryn

Him

She didn't sleep that night. I didn't rest either.

She listened to music, and, in my head, I started to put together a mixed CD for her. I don't know what she was listening to, but it doesn't matter. She will love what I give her.

Coming up with a mixed CD will probably amuse me for like, what, two days? I've come up with mixed CDs in here before while I was whittling away all those years before she came, soundtracks to empty days in this shithole. It gave me comfort before.

I start pulling ideas out of my head and making a mental note:

"Fine Again" by Seether

"Heaven's a Lie" by Lacuna Coil

"Going Under" by Evanescence

"Dig Lazarus Dig" by Nick Cave and the Bad Seeds

"Rama Llama" by Sons and Daughters

"Heart-Shaped Box" by Nirvana

My mind goes blank after only half a dozen songs. I can't even write any of this down. I've tried to pick up one of the notepads that takes up space in my box-prison, but my hand goes through it every time. I have no strength. This is the most utterly useless I've felt in a long time.

I reach out to the house, begging it to listen to me. I beg it to give her a sign that I'm here and I'm listening.

The best the house can do is a dripping tap in the bathroom.

The irony is disgusting.

Today, she's out at school. While I've been thinking up musical love letters, her mother has been banging around the house all day. I have no idea what she's supposed to do for work. Sounds like a lot of nothing. She's never on the phone, she never has anyone over, and she never sounds like she's doing anything worthwhile.

She's been moving furniture in what sounds like my parents' old bedroom for the last few hours. It honestly seems like she's just moving it, thinking a bit, then moving it right back. It's ridiculous.

In these last few days, she doesn't seem even remotely interested in checking the attic, where I've been waiting for someone to find me. Maybe today I can change that. I muster up all the strength I can and thump on the bottom of my cardboard box. It's a pitiful little sound. I doubt she heard anything over the scraping of something heavy and wooden. This place has made me weak.

I try again, a little louder this time. No reaction.

As I make my third bang, I'm angry and frustrated and bloody sick of this stupid box. I thump and the furniture stops moving. She heard that one.

I wait and eavesdrop on her as she steps out into the hallway. The bangs have left me tired. I don't know if I have another one in me. I think if I could sweat, the box would be soddened right now.

Please, I beg her mother. Please hear me.

Emma Kathryn

I wait and listen to the silence.

Eventually, she decides that the noise was nothing—that I was nothing. She goes back to her game of bedroom Tetris.

She's just as oblivious as my own mother was. In that moment, I decide that I hate her.

Chapter Three

Flora

Things I learned in school today:

One: The real name of the guy who used the word "Dude" is Phil.

Two: Phil likes to use the word "feminazi".

Three: Phil likes to use the word "feminazi" like he's only recently picked it up and is afraid that he'll forget it if he doesn't use it often.

How did I learn these things? Well, it would appear that Phil found me on Twitter and Instagram and didn't like some of the things I posted on there. It probably didn't help that my bio on both of these read: *"Flora – not a plant. Feminist with a passion for storytelling and no time for your nonsense. She/her."* Unfortunately, I've now become known as *"That Feminazi That Lives in the Murder House"*.

Emma Kathryn

Amazing.

I stopped checking my notifications around morning break. I also reluctantly set my Twitter account to private. My group chat was still on mute. I was contemplating leaving the group altogether, but that felt a bit too final. I was still naïve enough to think that Lucy would dump Dani and come up and visit me on her next available weekend.

I threw my phone into my tiny locker and dragged myself through classes for the rest of the day. After a full day of having no phone to look at, I was starting to feel as though I had chopped my own arm off. When I returned to pick it up at the end of the day (still nothing in the group chat), I was greeted by the goth girl from the day before, who was propping open the locker right next to mine. Her face lit up as I approached her apprehensively.

"Well, hey there, new girl," she beamed. Black lipstick hugged her lips, which opened to reveal incredibly white teeth. She looked as if she wanted to eat me.

"Hey yourself," I grunted, wondering if she would leave if I hid in my locker.

"I can't believe you live in Misery Mansion," she gushed, sliding around me to get a peek in my locker. There was nothing much to see after only two days of classes. "And that you have the locker right next to mine!"

I stopped and tried to think of the mousy girl who had tried to avoid eye contact next to me this morning. This was not her. I pointed to the locker she was now opening. "That's not your locker," I said indignantly.

"Sure is." She smiled, brandishing an open locker door covered with tiny cut-outs of cinematic vampires. Brad Pitt, Tilda Swinton, and Bela Lugosi all bared their fangs from behind clear sticky tape.

"What happened to the girl I saw here this morning?"

"I ate her," she said matter-of-factly.

"How did she taste?" I played along.

"Bitter."

I slammed my locker closed, signalling that this conversation was over. "Goodbye, Vampire Girl."

"Lydia." She smiled again, baring her own insubstantial fangs.

"Flora," I told her, almost against my better judgement.

"Oh, I know," she said as I walked away.

There was a brief fleeting moment where I wished she'd stayed longer. Lydia, the goth girl, seemed like she wanted to talk to me. Why couldn't I just shout out and ask her for her number? Lucy was apparently done with me, and I was going to have to settle here eventually. Something inside longed for Lydia to turn around again and offer to walk to class with me.

Please turn around, I silently begged. *Please. Let somebody in this town give a damn about me.*

I watched as she walked away with a swish of her dark hair. I said nothing and let her go.

The forty-minute walk home felt like an hour-and-forty-minute walk. This time, I didn't stop to talk to Mum when I got in. Instead, I stormed by her and went straight to my room. This time, I made sure to hang my blazer up inside my wardrobe.

Fuelled by rage and a lack of sleep, I proceeded to unpack with wild abandon. The sight of cardboard boxes suddenly sickened me, and I had to be rid of them. It wasn't as if keeping everything packed would suddenly force Mum to move back home. She wasn't going to walk into the room, see the boxes and say, "Ah well, since you're still packed, we might as well move back to Glasgow." I was being ridiculous keeping them like this for as long as I had.

The first thing to be done was to set up my speakers and plug in my phone. These days, that was all it was good for: music. I blasted something raw and angry—Nick Cave and the Bad Seeds. One of Dad's favourites.

I ripped open box after box of books and started sorting them into stacks: horror, fantasy, and young adult. I stacked each pile higher as my anger grew. Angry at Phil. Angry at his followers (both physical and digital) who tweeted zombie GIFs at me all day and groaned at me in the halls. Angry at Lydia, the goth girl who switched lockers just to mock me. Angry at Dad for not having called even once since we got here.

I pulled the next few books out of the box I was working on. These were Mum's novels: historical romances about ladies-in-waiting who were actually spies who then fall in love with the men they were supposed to monitor, or stories about warrior queens who fall in love with the captain of the guard. Basically, the formula was the following: strong woman meets handsome man, her principles are called into question, she learns how to juggle them, and a happy ending ensues. Mum's books all had happy endings—not one had a sad or even ambiguous ending. I used to consider this optimistic, but now, I saw it as foolish.

I threw the three books angrily towards my bedroom door. Two skidded across the floor and the third smacked the door hard, rattling the wood in its frame. Mum would have heard that, but I didn't care.

The next books out of the box were even worse. It was the *Archival Cycle* trilogy—my favourite fantasy series and the one which Dad had been commissioned to turn into a TV show. I stared at the covers, each painted with hues of green and brown. I'd read each book at least five times. Each read-through was faster than the last. Once, I'd even blitzed them all in a weekend. Opening the front cover of Book One, there was an inscription from the author, Mags Carter, whom I'd met at the Edinburgh Book Festival one year. I'd gushed to her and asked a question at the Q and A session after her reading. She was a writing rock star to me.

For the first few months of Dad's time in London, as he read through sample scripts and picked his writer's room, I tricked myself into thinking that he'd picked this project because he knew how much these books meant to me. Now, I realised that we had never had an actual conversation about these books. They'd sold millions of copies worldwide. It was really only a matter of time before it was adapted into something. Thankfully, the adaptation was a TV show and not a film (it would've been hacked to pieces in the cinema). It just happened to be my dad who was chosen for it.

And now, my favourite books had taken him away from me.

No. He'd taken himself away. But he'd taken my favourite story with him, scarring it with heartache and loneliness.

Again, I threw the books across the room.

This time, the door opened, and Mum stepped into the room. The books landed at her feet, and she gasped.

"Bloody hell, Flora, what are you playing at?" she barked, jumping back to avoid projectile fiction. "What is this?" She bent down and picked up two books at random. One was hers, and the other was the final part of the *Archival Cycle*.

"Nothing," I grumbled and started to break down the now empty box. There was something therapeutic about ripping the tape off the bottom. It was loud and obnoxious and drowned out the sound of Mum.

"Do we need to talk?" Mum asked, folding her arms and pressing the books against her chest.

I exhaled noisily. "About what, Mum? About the fact that Dad left us for fame and fortune? About the fact that you yanked us out of Glasgow and dropped us north of nowhere? Or maybe about the fact that you haven't written a goddam word since the divorce was finalised?"

A short staring contest ensued. I watched Mum try to grasp for an answer that was both sassy and motherly. I could see that she desperately wanted to pursue the sassy route, and my eyes dared her to. A fight was what I needed right now. I couldn't yell at my cruel classmates or at my former friends. However, I could certainly yell at Mum, who was standing right there at the threshold of my new domain.

We each stood our ground. The deep and guttural sounds of Nick Cave crooned over the stoic scene playing out. I wasn't backing down.

That meant that Mum had to. Resigning, she put the books down on my bedside table. Her fingers lingered a little on the cover of her own novel. It had a sticker on the cover bearing the words "Richard and Judy Book Club." She sighed.

"When you're ready for dinner, you can make something yourself," she said before storming out and leaving the door wide open. She knew I hated that. She also knew that it would make me follow her to close the door.

I suddenly felt awful. Watching her walk away made me feel a bit sick, like there was a serpent lashing around in my stomach. Mum and I didn't talk to each other like this. Yeah, we'd throw around a bit of sass and sarcasm, but we very seldom came close to actually hurting each other. I'd messed up. Bad.

I could either slam the door and shut Mum out even more, or I could follow her and make up.

Muttering to myself, I stormed across the room and grabbed at the door handle. Before I had the chance to do anything, an almighty bang rang out above my head. It shook the room. Tiny flecks of plaster fluttered loose from the ceiling and drifted down onto my bedsheets. I paused where I was and glanced out into the hall.

"FOR THE LOVE OF GOD, FLORA! STOP BANG-ING!" Mum yelled from downstairs, confirming her where-abouts in the house. This only made things stranger. Stepping out into the hallway, I glanced upwards and discovered a pull-string that was attached to a hatch in the ceiling.

Back in my room, my music began to skip. One line played through and looped three times, the word "upstairs" screaming in repeat from the speakers. I was streaming my music straight from Spotify; I'd never heard it glitch like this before. Our internet still wasn't very steady here—maybe it was the Wi-Fi dropping out. When the song corrected itself, I couldn't help but step into the hallway and stretch up. The pull-string was within reach. I grabbed it and pulled it down.

With a screech, a ladder descended from above. I stepped back and surveyed my new find. The words "murder house" danced in my brain to the tune of *The Best of Nick Cave and the Bad Seeds*. "Dig, Lazarus, Dig" came to a close, and "Lovely Creature" began. I love this song. Taking this as a sign, I pushed onwards and began to climb the stairs.

At the top, I poked my head through to discover dusty darkness. I breathed in and got a mouthful of age and abandon. Coughing, I covered my mouth until the dust settled. Opening the hatch must have disturbed everything. In front of me, a different cord dangled. Pulling on it, I was filled with relief as a single light popped into life. It lit the attic space in a sickly yellow glow. The light's influence didn't extend into the far reaches of the space and darkness filled the spots where the slanting roof met the floor. A few items littered the attic. Old paintings and dust sheets and a set of luggage. None of them would have made the noise I heard though.

On turning round, I discovered there was only one thing in the room, suggesting that this was the source of the noise. Sitting out on its own, with a mushroom cloud of dust floating above it, was a cardboard box. It was quite clear that it had been placed here recently as shown by all the dust disturbed around it. Luckily, it sat just within the circle of light created by the lightbulb, and I crouched down to see what it was.

Scrawled on one of the slightly open flaps was the name "Miles." I mouthed it. Then I said it aloud, just to see how it sounded coming from my lips. There was no dust on top of the box, as if it had been regularly handled and lovingly protected. Running my fingers over the edge of the opening, I contemplated whether or not I should open it.

Murder house. Murder house. Murder house.

As the voice of Nick Cave floated up through the ceiling, I damned myself for being such a feartie and I opened the box and began to explore.

"Well, hey there, Miles," I said as I was confronted by a treasure trove belonging to someone who had clearly been a teenage boy.

A bundle of CDs, a yearbook, a bottle of aftershave, a leather jacket, and a collection of notebooks all stared up at me. The yearbook was the obvious choice, and I plucked it from the collection.

The front cover read *Blairness High* 2006 and displayed the school crest which was embroidered onto my own school blazer. I flicked through the pages and saw a school that mostly reflected my new one but seemed a lot looser on the uniform policy. Not a blazer was to be seen, but barely tied ties and barely buttoned shirts were everywhere. Mum would never have ever let me out of the house like this.

Pictures showed students huddled together in group hugs on skiing trips (all wearing Ugg boots, of course, and a disproportionate amount of fake tan for a skiing trip), school dances where everybody looked like a member of Destiny's Child (so many pairs of giant hoop earrings), and a drama club which seemed to be putting on a performance of *Grease* (a show that I am sure they have probably done at least five times in the years since). I smiled and admired the happy faces looking out at the camera. It was strange seeing hallways that I kind of recognised, but from long before my time. Flicking further, I skimmed past the teacher's pages, only seeing three or four familiar faces.

Moving on, I came to the section I was searching for. Individual photos of each year-group. I had no idea where I would find the owner of this book, so I studied each image carefully. As I came to the seniors, I finally found who I was looking for: Miles Allen. Black-lined eyes gazed at me, and I touched the page absent-mindedly. Miles was not smiling—instead, he grimaced. He wore a long-sleeved grey t-shirt under his school shirt, and his tie was covered with safety pins. So goth. I rolled my eyes and let the book slam shut.

Returning to the box, I flicked through the CDs. Evanescence, Green Day, My Chemical Romance, Marilyn Manson, Cradle of Filth... If his guy-linered face hadn't given him away, I certainly would have thought goth by his music taste. At the bottom of the CD stack were three old Nick Cave albums. I picked them up and opened the CD cases. CDs looked foreign to me; I had almost all of my music on MP3, and the only CDs I'd ever really come across were the ones Dad would play in the car when I was little. Inside each of the cases in my hand was a little slip of paper. They had lyrics written on them, but they weren't in the right albums. For some unknown reason, this greatly annoyed me. Determined to right this wrong, I put the notes into the album their matching song was from. This made me feel much better. Putting them back, I scoured the box more.

The bottle of aftershave was only half-full, and I was surprised that it had lasted this long. I opened the lid and sprayed some carelessly into the air. A strong, musty smell enveloped me, and it was almost as comforting as correcting the lyrical mix-up. I held the bottle to my face and breathed in the forcefully masculine scent. I returned it to where I found it, placing it into the folds of the leather jacket that was lining the box.

Grasping the final items, I brought the notepads out. They were graffitied beyond belief with logos of bands from the early 2000s. Flicking through, I discovered more song lyrics, most of which I did not recognise. Some of them looked like poetry rather than song lyrics. I started to read one of the poems. It seemed fuelled by darkness, rage, and, oddly enough, raw passion...

Across the room, something creaked. Up until now, I had felt fine in the yellow glow of the lightbulb, but I suddenly felt uneasy. The dark edges of the room were moving closer as a sick feeling swelled in my stomach. Glancing back towards the box, I made a very quick decision. I grabbed one of the notepads and the yearbook. I left everything else where it was. Fleeing from the attic, I didn't even close the box—I just ran. I threw the stairs back up from whence they came and bolted into my room.

Spotify had finished my playlist and had decided to suggest something similar. I didn't want similar—I needed something different. I went for some rock, specifically Greta van Fleet. The lead singer began to screech the words "oh my" repeatedly as I shoved my new findings under my bed. They remained there for the rest of the night, mostly ignored until I lay in bed and tried to remember if I had turned the attic light off or not.

Him

. . .

Emma Kathryn

She says my name as if we've always known one another.

The figure of a teenage girl hunches over the box. She's short and slender. Her hair is dark and wild. I want to bury my face in it. A sprinkling of freckles decorates her cheeks. She's wearing a Blairness High uniform, but somehow still makes it look good.

I stay in the shadows of the attic, standing up straight and tall for the first time in what felt like an eternity. My knees are weak, like I could fall over at any moment. I look down at my right hand; my left refuses to move, still hanging limply at my side.

Words hang in my mouth, clinging to my tongue and refusing to leave. I want to call out to her. Nothing happens.

Everything feels strange now that I'm out in the open. The light from the bulb is too bright, too brash, too abrasive. I raise my one good arm, protecting my frail eyes from the violent glow. It does nothing. Light passes through my hand with ease.

Flora fumbles with my things. Her fingers probe my belongings and pluck out a yearbook. She strokes the pages and taps the hardback cover in time to the music that floats up from the bedroom.

I don't know how I've managed to get her up here. I'd listened to her getting angrier and angrier, and it made me mad too. I felt her rage and let it flow through me. She had called to me with her fury, and I'd answered.

I watch as she touches my CDs and douses herself in the scent of my aftershave. Now her hair smells like me—I've marked my territory without even trying. Edging around the room, I take in every detail of her face, watching her explore what has been my entire world for the last fifteen years. She's beautiful. Dark hair and dark eyes, just like the one whose name doesn't deserve to be said. Delicate hands thumb through the pages of my journal.

I want her to read it all. I want her to understand me. But what I really want is for her to see me—

Somehow, the floor creaks underneath me, and I shrink back. Her head whips around, and I swear, she looks right at me. A long minute hangs in the murky air between us.

Then something inside her snaps and she gathers up something from the box before closing the flaps over and scurrying down the ladder. The hatch closes behind her, and I'm alone again.

No. I'm not alone now.

Flora has just set me free.

Chapter Four

Flora

I tucked the yearbook into my bag as I readied myself for school. Another drizzly day was upon us, and I had the good sense to wear a hoodie under my blazer this time. I pulled the hood up and worked my way through the bad weather. Every day since moving here, Mum has offered me a lift to school, but I honestly can't think of anything worse than everyone seeing my mum waving me off at the school gates like I'm six years old. Plus, she'll get exceptionally nosy and try to insist on saying hello to everyone. Nobody needs that, especially not the girl who's been mocked incessantly all week.

My bag felt heavy, like I was carrying something either very precious or very dangerous. Something either made of glass or explosives—maybe even a glass explosive. Every now and then, I pressed my hand to my bag, checking that the book was still there, even though there was nowhere it could go.

No cars drove down the road to town this morning. This seemed unusual, considering that it was nearly half-eight on a weekday. Surely even the tiny people of this tiny village had places of work to go to. I tried not to think too deeply on this and enjoyed the lack of splashing and wall-crushing.

I still felt back for the way I spoke to Mum yesterday. As I walked, I thumbed my way through Amazon and tried to find something that said, "I'm sorry for being a terrible daughter". I settled on a little *"Grow your own herb garden"* kit because I knew she'd be missing our garden back in Glasgow. She had that garden looking ace. I was definitely not the only one missing home. I hit "Add to Basket" and added a little note saying *"Sorry I screwed up and thank you for your sage advice. Next thyme, I won't throw books at you."* When it arrived, I'd have to come up with a new way to apologise for the puns.

Once in school, I had the strange need to touch the book every time I had to open my bag for something. It felt like a magnet was drawing my fingers towards it. Even when I wasn't touching it, I kept my bag as close to me as I could. This book was my secret window to the past, and no one around me knew that I could look through it anytime I wanted.

Phil's stupid comments didn't seem to matter today. Somehow, I'd missed Lydia, Queen of the Goths, when I'd stopped by my locker. For the first time in a while, I entirely forgot about my group chat silence. In fact, I was happy to ignore them.

Instead, I thought about song lyrics and Miles' black-and-red-rimmed eyes—my own little Green Day wannabe, hidden in the past. Every now and then though, a little sense of sadness crept over me, and I remembered the words "Murder House";

it was highly likely that Miles Allen was the boy who had lived—and died—in my house. He suddenly seemed very lonely, and something in my chest lurched at this miserable idea. Maybe he would have understood how I've been feeling this week.

At lunch, I threw some food down my throat and retreated to the library; basically, the only place I knew that I could go and not be bothered. There were only two other people occupying desks in the library: a girl surrounded by science textbooks and a younger boy who was playing a handheld console with headphones in. The boy's head bobbed and swooped as if he were avoiding invisible obstacles, and the girl looked quite clearly distressed. Maybe she had a test next period.

I left her to it and went to the desk that was furthest away. It was near the window where I could see the rain slapping against the glass. Tucking my earbuds into my ear, I let some hipster boy band croon into my head. I pulled the old yearbook out and placed it on my lap. I stroked the cover as if I were Gollum keeping the One Ring safe from those pesky Hobbitses. Amongst the music in my ears, I thought I heard whispering. No words were audible, just the idea that someone was trying to talk to me. I pulled my earbuds out and stared at my phone. It displayed that it was playing Bastille, and my signal was strong. I wiped my earbuds and blew into it, just in case there was some dust or something else in them. Tucking them back in, the hissing noise was gone.

I opened the yearbook and found pictures of the library on World Book Day. Glancing around, I recognised the library. Its structure had not changed, but the books had changed quite dramatically. Copies of *Eragon* and *Wicked* had been replaced with *The Hate U Give* and the *Grishaverse* books, as well as an impressive display of the *Archival Cycle* books. In the photographs, teachers and students were dressed as famous characters in fiction. In the group picture, there were at least three Harry Potters (that had aged badly), a Sherlock Holmes, and an Oompa-Loompa. In the very back, a goth couple stood, one quite clearly Dracula and the other what I'm assuming was supposed to be Lucy, complete with faux-bitemarks on her neck. They were the only people not smiling. I instantly recognised Dracula as Miles.

"Oh my, that's a long time ago indeed," a voice said over me.

I jumped and yanked my headphones out, hurting my ears in the process. The librarian stood over me, smiling and grasping a cup of tea. Her glasses were perched partway down her nose in true, stereotypical librarian fashion.

"Sorry for startling you, dear," she said, patting me gently on the shoulder.

"It's okay," I mumbled, turning my music off.

"May I?" she asked, gesturing towards the book.

Something in my head hissed the word 'no', but I found myself handing it over to the warm-faced woman beside me. In that pushy, teachery way, she moved my bag from the other seat and sat down. I knew she didn't mean anything by it, but I'd spent all day being so protective of my bag that watching her move it sent waves of anxiety through my stomach.

"That was a good World Book Day," she said with a smile. "It's been years since we've done one."

Emma Kathryn

Finding my voice, I asked, "Why don't you do them now?"

"Not allowed to take an entire year-group off timetable anymore. Not even for an afternoon," she sighed. "And it's so much harder to find senior volunteers now. Everyone's coursework seems to have doubled."

I pointed to the vampire couple at the back. "Is that who these are? Senior volunteers?"

I watched her face change as her eye met the glare of Miles and his vampire victim. "The girl was," she said. "The boy showed up on the day, and I couldn't get him to go back to class. Stephanie. Her name was Stephanie, and she was a great help in the library. Came to book club, writers' group, and just got stuck in and helped however she could. I really liked her."

"What about the boy?" I took the book back from her and flicked to the page I had now become very familiar with. "Miles Allen?"

"Hmph," the librarian sighed. "Miles wasn't very well."

"What happened to him?"

She looked at me and cradled her mug of tea in her hands. I could see her studying my face and trying to work me out. "I'm afraid that Miles died," she said, eyes filled with sadness. "Only a short while after this book was printed."

"I thought as much," I said, closing the book over and going back to staring at the cover.

The librarian continued to watch me. "Am I right in saying that you're new?" she asked, trying to graze over the sad topic.

I nodded. "You're Shirley James' daughter, aren't you? Flora?"

Now it was my turn to sigh. I pushed the yearbook away after being swiftly brought back to the present with my own problems. "That's me," I said.

"That must be exciting," she smiled again.

"It would be if she would actually start writing again," I groaned.

The librarian nodded, as if she understood something that she could have absolutely no understanding of at all. "That must be difficult," she agreed.

"You have no idea."

"Do you write?" she asked me.

I was taken aback. While it would be presumptuous to assume that a writer's daughter must be a writer too, it was the first time I'd been asked this.

"Sometimes," I shrugged, trying to hide the fact that I'd been creating my own manuscripts since I could grasp a pencil. Granted, they were mostly badly drawn picture books with absurd and badly spelt captions back then.

"And I'd guess that you're a reader too?" she asked.

"What gave me away?" I scoffed.

This, she smiled wider at. "Well, most people like to spend their lunches lurking in the cafeteria or vaping behind the bin sheds. You chose the library."

I nodded and started picking awkwardly at my nails.

"We have the YA Book Club during Wednesday lunchtimes and Writers Group on Monday evenings. I'd love to see you come along to one."

"Maybe," I said half-heartedly. Part of me thought that this was a great idea; the other part thought that this would set me up for more torment, but this time at the hands of pretentious Chuck Palahniuk wannabes.

"I mean it," the librarian smiled. "I'm Mrs. Newman, and I'm sure the rest of the group would love to hear a new voice."

"Thank you," I told her. She stood up to go back to her lunch.

As she walked away, she glanced back at the yearbook. "I know that you've moved into a house with a very intriguing past," she added as an epilogue to our conversation, "but there's no good in looking back. It might be best if you put this back where you found it."

I nodded, but we both knew that I didn't mean it.

Sliding the book back towards me, I tucked it into my bag. I could leave now that I had Scooby-Doo'd up the information I needed, but I didn't. Instead, I pulled a notebook out of my bag and continued with a short story I'd been working on. The girl who was feverishly studying the science books watched Mrs. Newman disappear back into her office and then looked my way.

"Hey," she said, brushing away a wave of perfectly curled blonde hair. I looked around, just in case she meant the kid with the Nintendo. It was quite clearly me and I was being an idiot. "You're the Feminazi that lives in the Psycho House, right?"

This was a girl calling me a feminazi now. A girl. I couldn't get my head around it.

"That guy who lived in your house like mega-killed himself," she sneered. When I gave no response, she turned back to her books.

Something inside me already sort of knew this. I can't explain why or how. The book in my bag called to me, but now, I didn't want to look at it. I hated myself for even bringing it with me this morning. What was I thinking? Something sang out to me—a call, a pulse, a cry. I ignored it. Or at least, I did my very best to.

I gathered up my things and left the library. I didn't know where to go. The rest of lunch was spent wandering aimlessly around corridors I had already familiarised myself with from fifteen-year-old photographs.

Him

Walking comes back to me like riding a bike. Part of me was scared that I'd be forever crammed in that box or that if I did get out, I'd be slithering along the floor, pulling myself along with that one good arm.

I slide through walls and doors and floors with ease. I can step from one room to another without any effort at all. The house has opened up to me, and I take from it what I need.

The first night, I walked around the whole house, taking in the changes. Books filled the room we used to have silent dinners in. The kitchen seemed warm, even hours after they'd finished cooking in it. I looked at pictures pinned to a noticeboard. A mother and daughter smiled back from a theme park with sparkly mouse ears on their heads. This looked like it had been a long time ago now. There were certainly no mouse ears in this house when I lived here.

Part of me detests how busy the rooms seem, crammed full of stuff, all of it holding a story behind it—the story of their life before this house. I want to crush the boxes and throw them all out. There had never been so many stories in this house.

There had only ever been one story—my story.

Everyone else had given it a bad ending.

This is my chance though. My chance to write a game-changing sequel. Set the record straight. Tell it my way.

Today I get a good look at the mother, who is still perpetually moving furniture. She looks like Flora thirty years from now. Stress has done a bit of a number on her, and there's stringy sections of grey through her dark hair. Once she finally stops rearranging things, she retires to the dining room. It's supposed to be a library, but I can't see it as anything other than the room where my father used to yell across the table at my mother and me.

There's a desk in here instead of a dining table. She's got a laptop open on it, and it looks like she's attempting to write something. There are only a few paragraphs in the Word document, and she's fidgeting her way through writing anything more than that. In fact, the project is so fresh, it's still titled "Document One". She hasn't even bothered to save it yet.

I've been listening to Flora rage at her mother for days now. Writing comes up frequently in their arguments and snide, snippy comments. From what Flora has been saying, it had seemed like her mother wasn't writing at all.

From here, it looks like she's trying.

My mother had given up by the time the bad things happened. It's not fair. Jealousy and frustration tug at my empty chest.

Her head perks up, as if an idea has struck her. She pushes her glasses further up the bridge of her nose, and suddenly, she types faster than she has all day. Her silver-painted nails dart across the keyboard. She's on a roll.

I glide over to the bookshelves. I know exactly what I'm looking for. She's made it easy for me—the majority of her book collection is in alphabetical order, but her own books have a shelf to themselves. What a narcissist.

There are five different titles, but she's got a couple of different copies of each. I glance at the spines and run my finger along them. Some are hardback and some have fancy covers. One of them bares a French translation of the title on its spine.

I pick one of the paperbacks and push it off the shelf. It lands on the floor with a soft thud, and the pages bend. She spins her head round and darts out of her seat. She can't let her precious book get ruined.

She picks it up and flattens the folded corner of one of the pages. A flicker of annoyance and disappointment crosses her face before she carefully puts it back on the shelf.

I let her return to the desk before making my next move. She adjusts her glasses and reads for a moment. Then her fingers twitch and she begins to type again. For a moment, it seems like she's picking up momentum, getting into the flow, finding her grove...

THUD.

Emma Kathryn

I knock the same book to the ground again. More pages bend and the cover folds.

"Bloody hell!" her mother yells, standing quickly.

There's a moment where she stares at the floor, unable to believe what's going on. She smoothes down a crease in her navy dress, sliding her hands over the printed silver stars on the fabric. Then, she rescues the book. I stand over her as she frets at the poor pages. She's so short, just like Flora. I laugh a little and she snaps up, standing straight.

I stop laughing. She heard me! A grin spreads across my face. This is tiring me out, but it's still the best I've felt all day. The strain to move the books is a lot, but watching this makes it worth it.

The woman looks around and slides the book back into place. I watch as she sits back at her desk and shakes her head. She takes a big swig of coffee from a mug on the table. As she sets it back down, it rattles a little—she's shaking. It's hard not to laugh again.

Once more, I let her start typing. The adrenaline from the fright has clearly buoyed her up. She's put away several paragraphs since I followed her in here. In fact, I'd say there's actually a full page of writing here, maybe even two. I read none of it. I don't even remotely care what drivel she's putting down on the page. Instead, I wait.

As I see her hit page three, I decide that's enough. I pick a different book this time—one of her hardback copies. It hits the wooden floor with an almighty bang. This time she yelps as she jumps.

She doesn't move straight away. She stares at the bookshelf and then the floor, trying to calculate what's wrong with the shelf. Maybe it's at an angle? Maybe she didn't assemble it correctly? Maybe it's the soul of the boy who died in this house because his own mother didn't bother to check on him?

When she gets up, I make a move. I've spent this entire episode calculating. Shifting the books has taken a lot of energy but I need to do this last thing. While she stands at the bookcase and picks up the crappy romance novel, I go to her laptop and hit "Close" on Word. A warning flashes up, reading "Save your changes to this file?".

I hit my answer. "No."

The program shuts down, and I'm greeted with her laptop wallpaper. It's a picture of her and Flora sharing an obnoxiously large ice cream sundae. They're both laughing like they've just heard the funniest joke ever.

She's put the book back by now and has returned to the desk. There's a beat and then she realises what she's looking at.

"What?" she says to herself as she lowers herself back in her seat. "No."

Yes.

"No, no, no. This is the best thing I've done in months."

You should have saved it then, you idiot.

There's a real look of exasperation on her face and she slams the laptop shut. She grabs the coffee cup and storms towards the kitchen. I don't follow her—I don't need to. I've gotten what I need from this, and it was bloody brilliant.

Emma Kathryn

Now that she's out of the room, I've got one last thing I want to try. I know I've got time. She's just lost an hour's worth of work, and she's not going to even look at her laptop for the rest of the day.

I drag the crumpled paperback off the shelf and flick it open to a random page. With great effort, I tear it out. The noise is incredibly satisfying, even though I'm exhausted and nearly spent. I tear another.

And another.

And another.

Then I put the book back on the shelf and take the pages with me. This is going to be a lot of fun.

Chapter Five

Flora

By the time the weekend came around, Mum and I were talking to each other again—I reckon it was the herb puns that fixed it. The yearbook was under my bed with the notepads, and I was doing my best not to think about Miles Allen, the Suicide Teen of Mockingbird Lane.

Mum was still not writing, but she had decided that her time would best be spent "reconnecting" with me over the weekend. On Friday night, we watched reruns of *Will and Grace*. We ordered pizza from the local chippy because there wasn't a Domino's or Pizza Hut for miles. More wine was drunk, along with some vodka she'd forgotten that she'd had. Once she'd reached the point of no return, I stole a glass of vodka for myself, and then a second. She'd never know.

When she fell asleep on the couch, I escaped to my room. There's only so much of *Will and Grace* that you can watch back-to-back. Upstairs, I finally took my group chat off mute. There hadn't been any messages anyway. I'd officially been forgotten, and it was obvious that they'd all migrated to a new group chat—one I wasn't invited to.

I hit the *"Leave This Group"* button. I thought it would make me feel better. Instead, it felt hideously final.

Now that the weekend had come around, I decided that it was time to return to Twitter, but I safeguarded myself against further attacks by setting my profile to private. Having to do this irked me because it meant that sharing my tweets was now restricted to the 346 sad people who followed me. Hopefully, in a few weeks, I'd be able to put it back to public, but now even some of the girls at school were calling me Murder House Feminazi. How the hell do you compete with that?

I did notice one new follower of note. DeadGirlWalking had followed me one day ago. The pouting face of Lydia, Queen of the Goths, looked at me from her profile picture. I didn't follow back. Instead, I thumbed my way through her profile out of morbid curiosity. She shared lots of horror movie news, Kat Von D makeup, and videos from the Skater—who I could now see was called Charlie. They followed each other. Skateboarding Charlie had not tried to follow me. Considering my current lack of group chat, I followed my new locker neighbour. Maybe she wouldn't be that bad after all. Plus, I needed someone to talk to who wasn't just a yearbook picture of a dead kid.

Sighing, I flicked my light out and wriggled into bed. Staring up at the ceiling, I lamented my first week in the hellhole that was Blairness. This was so shit. I wanted to go home. I wanted my friends back. I wanted to see Dad. I wanted Mum back in that wild frantic writing/editing cycle that she was always so fun during.

I wanted anything but this place.

Tears pricked my eyelids. I felt profoundly alone. The prospect of tears turned into full-scale crying, and I held my pyjama cuffs to my face, attempting to catch the sadness and stop it from hitting the pillow. There was no holding it back, though—I gave in, sobbing hard and ugly.

Downstairs, a light switch clicked, and the TV turned off. I quickly tried to compose myself so that Mum wouldn't hear my crying. An intervention from Mum was the last thing I needed right now. It was also the last thing she needed, thinking her kid was a broken mess. I sat up in bed and wiped my face. Sniffing hard, I tried to pull my sorrow back inside and push it down deep.

As I pressed my head back against the headboard, I saw a familiar shape across the darkened room. I'd left my blazer on the handle of the cupboard again. I was not spending another night awake and staring at something that wasn't even remotely frightening again. Sighing, I flicked my lamp back on to take it down.

My blazer wasn't hanging from the handle—the leather jacket from the box in the attic was. I gasped and leapt from the bed. In one swift and near-impossible movement, I was out of bed, opening the bedroom door and in the hallway, keeping my eyes trained firmly on the phantom jacket. As I back-peddled in the hall, I back-peddled right into someone.

Screaming, I jumped around to discover Mum, also screaming, "Bloody hell, Flora, what is it?"

"Mum," I gasped, breath shuddering in my chest. "Mum, there's a jacket in my room." Heart pounding, I grabbed her arm, relieved that it was her but at the same time still reeling from the fright. This didn't change the fact that there was a dead boy's jacket in my bedroom.

"What?" Mum asked, face filled with tired, angry confusion.

"I found a jacket upstairs and it's in my room," I said, trying to remember how to breathe normally.

She stormed by me, partly filled with annoyance, but mostly filled with wine and a little bit of vodka. Sure enough, I hadn't imagined it—the scuffed and dusty leather jacket was hanging where I'd initially seen it.

"Oh my god, Flora, why does it smell like a teenage boy who's just discovered Lynx body spray in here?" Mum quizzed, waving at invisible stink lines wafting through the air.

I pointed at the jacket.

Without care or worry, Mum swiped it from its perch. "Where did this come from?" she asked. I could see her processing this and trying to work out if I'd been sneaking boys in the window for some late-night virginity-taking. The good thing is that, having a romance writer for a mother, Mum was very encouraging of formative steps in love and probably wouldn't even have freaked out (much) if there had been an actual boy in here. Plus, she trusted me—she knew that I wouldn't.

"I found it in the attic," I confessed, "but I left it up there. I promise. I didn't take this."

Mum glanced between me and the jacket and then looked out into the hall. "We have an attic?" she wondered aloud.

"Yes," I exhaled, suddenly raging that she'd drunk so much. "But I swear that I did not bring this jacket down."

"Right," Mum said, apparently not believing that a jacket had fallen through the ceiling and wound up hanging from my cupboard door. "Well, it's late, so how about I take this for just now and in the morning, we'll go upstairs and bin any rubbish that the last people left."

From under the bed, I imagined that the stolen items were whispering to me. This is what I got for stealing some of that vodka. I nodded.

"Okay then," Mum said, folding the jacket over her arm, and heading back into the hallway. "Nighty night, sweetie."

She staggered off to bed, and I closed my room door again. She never remembered to close that door.

My heart was still pounding. There was no way I was sleeping tonight. I climbed back into bed and pulled my knees up to my chest. The lamp stayed on for the rest of the night.

Chapter Six

Flora

In the morning, I woke to the sound of clanging and banging. Leaving my room in my pyjamas, I found the attic ladder down. My feet seemed to want me to climb it, but my head said that would be stupid. My stomach said to at least go find breakfast first.

The clanging and banging continued, but it seemed to be coming from downstairs. Whispering a quiet "thank God", I edged around the ladder and went to investigate. In the kitchen, the kettle was boiling and there were plates of pancakes prepared. It would seem that Mum was still on her "reconnect" plan. However, she was nowhere to be seen. The back door was open, and I shuffled out in my slippers to see where she was.

The garden was overgrown and wild, much like the little island in the middle of the lake that I had to walk around to and from school. Mum was where the bins were, trying to get her head around which bin was for what. She'd found the glass bin, which was no surprise considering that she had wine-related evidence to dispose of. I watched her open the blue bin and stare into the bottom.

"Cardboard," I told her with my arms folded across her chest.

I clearly gave her a fright, making her jump and seemingly giving her headache an extra boost. "Morning, sweetie," she winced, dropping the broken down "Miles" box into the bin. I spotted the leather jacket hanging over the side of the green general waste bin. Mum followed my gaze and swiftly tipped the jacket the rest of the way. "I've made pancakes," she said. Apparently, we were brushing last night off as something that wasn't worth mentioning. "But if you swipe any of my booze again, you're banned from both it and pancakes for good," she added with an angry finger jab in my direction.

"And how do you plan on policing this?" I asked, with a tone that was more apologetic than angsty.

"Guess we'll just have to live together for the rest of our lives." She sighed, ditching the last of the boxes' contents. I heard the aftershave hit something with an angry tinkling of glass. Mum swiftly closed the lid over before the smell assaulted us further.

"Ah Mum, we both know that my generation won't get to move out until we're pushing forty," I said, following her inside.

"Please don't," she said, closing the back door behind me.

Hands were washed, pancakes were served, and we both went about reading as we ate. Mum read *The Guardian* on her iPad, and I secretly flicked through *Archival Cycle* gossip on my phone. This was a tiny betrayal to Mum, but I hadn't looked last night, and I was scared that I had missed something. They had just announced that a newcomer, Janet Humphrey, was definitely playing the lead after a set photo revealed her joking with Thandiwe Newton. I had never heard of her, and her credits included some BBC drama in 2017, a teeny tiny part in *Game of Thrones* (which British actors *hadn't* been in *Game of Thrones* though?), and a radio adaptation of a Neil Gaiman short story last year.

The fan forums generally seemed excited. Someone was raving that they'd been tweeting that Janet should get the part for years (*sure, Jan*). Someone else was breaking down the photographs and musing that some of the props suggested a big B-plot that hadn't appeared until Book Two would be turning up earlier. A troll was complaining about the casting of Thandiwe Newton. Idiot. She was perfect for the High Priestess.

I studied the set photo, where Janet was in full costume and make-up but was holding a plastic water bottle and laughing. I guess it kind of matched the image I'd had of Ophie, the lead character, in my head, but the magic was ruined with the anachronisms. She was a bit Elle Fanning meets Sophie Turner. Another part of my love for these books was chipped away. Still, there were no pictures of Dad.

Mum insisted that we were going into the village for the day. I told her that, as someone who walks through it twice a day for school, there was no need for a whole day. We could easily wander round in about an hour. She insisted that this was nonsense and that we were going. She also insisted on taking the car, which I informed her meant that she was responsible for killing the planet. She suggested that I walk and she'd take the car. I accepted defeat and was subjected to listening to Michael Bublé in the car as an act of punishment. Surely it was a crime to listen to Michael Bublé outside of the festive period?

We parked in the world's tiniest car park (which somehow still had three empty spaces, so I used this to prove my point to Mum that no one needed a car in this stupid place), and Mum let me give the tour. I don't know how she'd managed a week here without going into the village. Where did she even get our food shopping from? First of all, Mum wanted to see where I went to school. Who knows why—it's not like there was anything to actually see on a Saturday. She ooh-ed and aah-ed like it was interesting. It wasn't. Next was a walk to the little café, where she decided we had to have lunch.

A wee old lady served us while a teenager leaned against the counter, tapping away at her phone.

"Do you know that girl?" Mum whispered to me in the least subtle way imaginable.

"Mum, I don't know all of the teenagers," I joked. "Assuming every teenager knows each other is outrageously ageist."

"You don't have to be such a smart mouth when I'm trying my best," Mum said, disappointed and letting my dazzling wit fly over her head.

"Sorry," I muttered and collected the tray with our lunch before I followed her to a table.

Emma Kathryn

I had a cheese toastie and a glass of Coke while Mum had a baked potato and a cup of coffee. We stayed in longer than I think the girl found socially acceptable. At one point, she quite clearly took a picture of us, so I'm certain that I'd been Snapchatted to some equally sullen folk.

As we ate, Mum asked me more about school. "Have you met *anyone* nice yet?" she asked.

She sat picking at the tuna on her baked potato, which had more mayonnaise in it than she found palatable. I could never understand how she could eat tuna on a baked potato. What was wrong with eating it with cheese and butter like the rest of us?

"Uhm..." I stalled, considering how truthful to be. I decided it was better to be honest—it was too small a village for lies. "The school librarian, I guess."

Mum grimaced and didn't even try to hide it. "Oh sweetie," she sighed. "You've got to put yourself out there more. You've been there a week. Have you even spoken to anyone at all?"

"An arsehole named Phil," I shrugged. "Some goth girl who stalks my locker. In fact, maybe she lives in there. Hangs upside down in it until she senses me coming along so she can spring out at me. And some girl in the library who also wanted to inform me of the torrid history of our lovely home, Mother."

Mum shook her head and finished her coffee. "We're going to be here for some time, Flora," she said after putting her empty cup down. "The least you could do is make some kind of attempt to settle in."

"Wise words," I sighed. "Super, super helpful. I'll remember that the next time any potential best friends walk by."

"No need to be sarcastic," she informed me before asking the old lady for the bill. She dragged me out without even letting me finish my glass of juice first. What a waste.

"And anyway," she continued as she pulled me out the door, "you read loads of Anne Rice novels last year. Maybe the vampire girl might be fun to talk to."

I didn't want to tell her that she was right, but I also didn't want to disappoint her any more than I already had. So, I just nodded as we stepped back into the daylight.

There was a sense of tension, as if she wanted to say something else. I couldn't help but feel like she was annoyed at me for something else, but I couldn't quite put my finger on what it was.

Out on the street, we passed a handful of people, most of whom were leaving the local church. Mum had somehow managed to time our visit into the village to coincide with church getting out, thus alerting the locals to our heathenistic ways of not attending. Mum strongly refused to believe in going to any kind of church, so she pulled me away quickly so as not to run into the vicar (or minister, or whatever name the spiritual leader here goes by). I couldn't help but wonder why the church was so busy on a Saturday morning. Surely these people don't spend their entire weekend praying?

Instead, we wound up on the High Street where a few little shops peppered the road. There was a tailor, a baker, and a cute little card shop. There was also some kind of small dance studio with full glass windows. We could see inside, and a woman was teaching a bunch of little girls how to do some steps that involved lots of stretching and spinning. Mum seemed to find this adorable and stopped to watch. I tried to warn her that there were probably laws against watching children stretch, but she told me to stop being crude and continued to grin through the glass like some kind of big creep.

As she watched, I shoved my hands in my pockets and tried to look like I wasn't actually with her. However, I allowed myself a quick look in and discovered that the Skater from my English class was sitting at the back of the studio, beside a music system. He was in skinny jeans and a T-shirt with a symbol on it that I instantly recognised: the green logo of the rebel poison makers of the Elven Herbalist Guild. It was an *Archival Cycle* reference, and it brought a grin to my face. Unfortunately, at this exact moment, he looked up and met my eyes. I did my best to drop the cheeser, but he let out a tiny smile himself and gave me a little wave.

Of course, Mum saw this.

"Who's that?" she asked, giving me a nudge and pulling my attention away.

"No one," I lied.

"Flora..."

"Just a boy from a couple of my classes." It had turned out we didn't just share English class, but history too.

This brought out the romance writer in Mum, and she started to beam like she'd just seen her first grandchild. "What's his name?!"

It was Charlie. "I don't know," I lied.

"How do you not know?"

"There are like twenty-something people in all of my classes," I reasoned. "I'm sorry if it takes longer than a week to pick up all of their names."

While we were arguing about how many names I had learned, the music had stopped inside, and the children were starting to leave. Peeking back, I could see the Skater talking to the obscenely beautiful woman who had taught the class. Their gestures seemed to mimic the ones my mum and I were using. Then the dance teacher started to walk towards the door. As a little kid shoved the door open, I could hear the Skater yell, "Mum, no!" as the woman presented a prize-winning smile and approached us outside.

"Well, hello there," she said with a broad Spanish accent.

Mum slapped on her Book Tour PR face and held her hand out. "Shirley James, lovely dance studio you have here," she beamed, taking the dancer's elegant hand and shaking it firmly.

"Sara Burns, and thank you very much," she said.

Charlie grudgingly took a step outside. We exchanged an awkward nod and a mumbled "hey".

"And this is my son Charlie," Sara added, pulling Charlie to the forefront.

"This is Flora," my Mum added, as if this was some kind of child-off.

"Yes, Charlie was telling me that there was a new addition to the village," Sara smiled.

"Oh my God, Mum," Charlie hissed.

"What?!" Sara continued to smile before turning to me. "He was saying that you were joining the library clubs?"

I froze a little. I hadn't told anyone anything about my meeting with Mrs. Newman, and I certainly hadn't decided on going. I probably wouldn't now. My eyes must have given away my sense of alarm because Charlie started frantically shaking his head.

"No no no, I totally didn't say that," he gushed. "It's just that Mrs. Newman had said that she'd met you and wanted someone to try and talk you into going to the writers' group."

I definitely wasn't getting an opportunity to speak because Mum took this chance to jump in. "You didn't tell me that you were joining a club! You should definitely join. You love writing," she said, somehow managing to maintain her fake smile and sound accusatory at the same time. "She loves writing," Mum repeated to Sara and Charlie.

"I hadn't decided on going yet," I said, trying to hide how enraged I was at every single person standing around me right now.

"Oh, well, you most definitely should," Mum said. She turned her attention to Sara and started to talk as if I wasn't even there. "I was telling her less than an hour ago that she needed to start making friends—"

"Bloody hell, Mum," I gasped.

"I mean, we've just moved here, and Flora isn't very good at meeting people."

"Mum!"

"Oh, trust me," Sara continued, "Charlie would be just as bad. It's all computer, skateboard, computer, skateboard..."

"Fuck's sake, Mum!" It was Charlie's turn this time.

"Language!" she yelled, then hissing something at him in Spanish.

"Language, Mum!" he nipped back with a smirk.

Sara stopped short of saying something else and plastered the fake smile back on. "Shirley, would you like to come in and see the studio? I do adult evening classes," she said, regaining her grace and poise.

"I would love to!" Mum said, giving me a stay-out-here-and-learn-to-make-friends face. There seemed to be an exchange going on between the mother and son beside us as well. The mums vanished inside and left the teens standing out on the pavement.

A moment of silence passed. I kept my hands firmly in my pockets. Charlie gave his mop of hair a quick brush out of his eyes.

"I'm really sorry," he eventually blurted out. "I promise that I'm not going around talking about you or trying to coax you into joining the library cult." A genuine apology fluttered across his face and he pulled at his clothes in a way that was both incredibly self-conscious and kind of adorable. "I swear to God, I'm not running about screaming 'We got one!' in a *Ghostbusters*-esque fashion. I promise."

A little laugh escaped me. I withdrew my hands from my pockets and anchored them to the strap of my bag, which hung over my shoulder. "That's okay. Mum seems to be offering me up to anyone that'll take me now anyway. Her biggest fear is that I'll die alone or that I'll never leave the house. Like, ever."

"Looks like our Mums have found their soulmates then," he said.

"Definitely," I responded.

Silence followed as we both struggled with something to say.

"So, how's your first week here?" he asked after finding the most obvious question he could.

"Kind of dire," I shrugged.

"Don't worry, it's like that all the time," he agreed.

"Oh, good. I was dreading the thought of it getting better," I said sarcastically.

"Well, it sucks permanently here, so you've got nothing to fear," he replied equally sarcastically.

"Excellent," I said. I felt a real smile rise to my lips. Luckily, his mouth seemed to match.

"I'm not a writer, by the way," he said. "Just in case you turn up at writers' group and expect me to be writing or something."

"Yeah, totally," I shrugged, continuing our snarky back and forth. "I mean, who would expect a writer at a writers' group?"

"Nah, I mean it," he replied. "I'm the website, podcast, vlogger guy."

I was honestly taken aback, and I don't think I hid it very well. "Ah. Okay. That's cool...I guess..."

"No, I'm not just some techie nerd that hangs out at school clubs looking for IT work. I mean, I *am* a techie nerd..." He stopped for a moment and ruffled his hair again. "My twin sister, Lydia, goes and volunteers me for stuff all the time."

Sister... Lydia, Queen of the Goths, was his twin sister.

"It's kind of her thing. She thinks everyone should be involved in anything she's involved with. Not that she's a nut job. She just has no filter. Anyway, she told Mrs. Newman I'd set them up a website, and I did, and then she told her I'd edit the radio play they all recorded, and I did. And now I go every week, and I think Mrs. Newman just comes up with crap for me to do because I'm always hanging around."

"That actually is kind of cool," I admitted. I still couldn't get over the fact that his twin was the vampire in the next locker.

"Meh." He shrugged again. "Something to put on university application forms, I guess."

"I only write," I smiled.

"Simpleton," he joked.

Another lull of quiet came. This one didn't feel so awkward though.

"You side with the Poison Makers?" I asked, pointing at his t-shirt.

As if forgetting what he was wearing, he looked down and the penny dropped. Suddenly, his face was animated, and his eyes glinted with that look Mum got when people asked her who was her favourite of Henry VIII's wives.

"Oh yeah," he said. His voice became way bubblier. "I mean, they're the real badasses of the series. You like the *Archival Cycle?*"

"Probably to an unhealthy extent," I answered. I unzipped my hoodie to reveal my t-shirt which read the words "*Blood does not make me yours*" across it.

"Nice. Does that make you a fan of the Guardians Guild?" he asked. That was the Guild that Ophie, the lead character, joined after leaving the Assassin's Guild when her father betrayed her.

I took a sharp intake of breath, preparing myself for the usual grief I took for my next response. "To be honest, I'd probably be an Elf Ranger. The site just didn't have those t-shirts."

"Oooooooh!" He snorted. "You fiend."

In the books, the Elf Rangers were deadly snipers who would have killed you before you even realised they were there. Most people hated them, but they were crucial in Book Three, and Ophie would never have broken the blood curse and stopped her father's war without them.

"I'm the worst," I laughed. "But I do like all the stuff with the Guardians. Book Three is great."

"I'm sorry, you lost me at 'I'm a dirty sniper'."

Without thinking, I gave him a playful nudge on the arm. Something crackled between us, and I instantly felt like an idiot. I had dropped my guard and taken a step too far. I couldn't even meet his eye.

"I better go," I said, pushing my hands back into my pockets.

Charlie, on the other hand, was still smiling. "Cool. I'll go try to separate our mums," he said and disappeared back inside.

Bloody hell, what was I thinking? He probably thought I was some kind of psychopath. Pretty sure I'd just blown my first chance of a pal here. I had punched him in the arm. I'd have just as well punched him square in the face. I couldn't possibly go to the writers' group now.

Well done, Flora, I thought to myself. *You've royally screwed this one up.*

A couple of seconds later, Mum emerged. She waved at Sara and Charlie through the glass. Charlie gave me a little wave, and I threw one back. Eugh, what had I done?

Mum, however, was positively ecstatic. She'd practically decided that she and Sara were lost sisters and talked about her the whole way back to the car. The whole way.

"Charlie's a twin!" Mum beamed as she threw her bag in the back seat with reckless abandon. "He's got a sister called Lydia! And she goes to the clubs too!"

"I know, Mum, she's the goth who lives in the locker next to mine."

"Isn't that just lovely?"

As I sat in the front seat and did up my seatbelt, Mum threw in one of those comments Mums always try to make when they think you're not listening so that you can't fight it: "So, I gave Sara your mobile number and we agreed that Charlie would text you to remind you about the writer's group and the book club and any of the other library events you might be interested in."

Emma Kathryn

"You did what?!"

Apparently, my mum was now my pimp.

Him

She's out with her mother, so I'm stuck in here alone. I didn't expect her to be out all day. My world is empty again—I don't like it.

The house makes settling noises, but none of them alarm me. I've been here long enough to recognise every tiny rattle and moan. I know the sounds of this house as if they're my invisible family. The creaking floorboards are my brothers, and the groan of the pipes are my sisters—siblings I never had in life.

But today, none of these noises comfort me. They just remind me that she's not here.

I contemplate following them. I remember the way back into town. I used to ride my bike to school. The bike is long gone, but my memory of the route is still fresh.

That's it. I'm going. I'll find her and her stupid mother and I'll spend the day with them, like a silent guide to Blairness. I hate this stupid town but, for her, I'd explore it if it meant staying by her side.

I move through the house, taking in the changes that have been starting to take shape. Her mother's stamp is everywhere. She leaves books lying at her arse and there are family pictures starting to appear in mismatching frames on every surface. I knock a few over as I pass. One of them lets out a satisfying crack as it hits the floor.

I slip through the front door, not worrying about keys or locks. There are a couple of plant pots on the porch. I walk past them and make my way into the front garden. Glancing back, I notice that the pots hold no plants. It's probably just due to the time of year, but I'm guessing they'll be bustling with life by summer. Everything my dad ever put on this porch died.

The large pond stretches out between me and the main road. It's not as stagnant as I expected it to be. There are actually some fish in it, and a few ducks mill about on the small island in the centre of the water. It's oddly peaceful.

Curiosity overcomes me and I step out onto the water, wondering if I'll get wet. I don't even break the surface and instead, walk across it with ease. A small snort escapes me. I can imagine everyone who ever called me a Satan worshipper at school would have loved this. I make it to the island, and the ducks scarper. The little ones panic as they try to escape me. Continuing, I cross the island and the rest of the water. The path to the main road awaits me.

Just as I prepare to step onto the road and escape this bloody house, an invisible wall stops me.

No, *I think.* No, not this.

I slide my hand over the imperceptible barrier. It holds me back and traps me on the grounds. I was afraid of this—afraid that I really would be stuck in this hellscape forever.

I punch at nothing as my excursion into town is cancelled.

Chapter Seven

Flora

When we got back home, I was pretty sure that I just wanted to curl up in a tiny ball under my bed and die. Not only had I punched a potential acquaintance in the arm, but my mum had tried to thrust my friendship upon him via his mother. I could imagine him binning my number and telling his sister not to bother with me.

Rushing upstairs, I aimed for a dramatic flop down on my bed à la actress in the 1920s or Disney princess, but was stopped when I discovered my bed was currently occupied. The notepad I had taken from the box upstairs, of which I was sure I had only taken one, had multiplied. The now-collection of notepads were spread across my bed with the year-book lying open in the very centre.

It was open at the picture of Miles.

Air froze in my lungs. I considered yelling for Mum to come look at this but, considering the jacket incident last night, I was pretty sure she wouldn't believe me. I had a choice: I could freak the hell out, or I could calmly attempt to deal with it. Something akin to crying threatened my eyes, but I fought it off.

Slowly and gingerly, I closed the yearbook, afraid that if I made any sudden movements, the book would bite me. Then, I gathered up the notepads and discovered that there were still only a few present, but the pages had been torn out and scattered. There was no way of knowing which pages were from which notepads, so I just tucked them into whatever ones fit and tried not to look at the wild handwriting.

It was difficult though. I tried my hardest not to look, not to read. However, the words called like a siren to a sailor. The whispering sound came back, and my head began to throb. Pages fell from my hands until I was holding only one page.

You're never going to love me.

Not like Narcissus loved himself.

I am Echo and you cannot hear me

Not over your own reflection.

Like Persephone, I am condemned to the underworld

And you're never going to save me.

I love you and I hate you.

You hate me and can't love me.

You'll never die for me.

Emma Kathryn

Not like I'd die for you.

Common sense kicked in, and I threw the page to the ground. It wasn't even a well-written poem. It was an angry scrawl from someone who had just Googled a bunch of myths and then just started screaming "I hate you" into the ether.

I scoffed and threw the papers back under the bed. "Shit," I muttered as I ditched it.

On the other hand, I couldn't stand to look at the yearbook anymore. I opened the cupboard (which was currently just full of boxes of clothes I had yet to sort) and chucked it as far back as I could.

As the yearbook landed on a bunch of old dresses I was probably never going to wear again, I noticed something else. There was a ball of scrunched up papers in here. I reached down to grab them and stepped out of the dark cupboard and into the light of my bedroom.

It was a bunch of pages torn out of a book. Confusion washed over me as I tried to recognise or remember why there would be ripped book pages in amongst my old clothes. When had I ever torn pages out of a book? That's sacrilege in this house. You don't hurt books. I wouldn't do it. Mum wouldn't do it. Hell, this time last year, even Dad wouldn't do it.

The numbers didn't match up, so it wasn't a section pulled out of a book. It seemed like random pages. I started to skim the words to see if I recognised what book it came from.

Oh, God. Realisation hit me like a tidal wave.

These were from one of Mum's books. The first one that got really popular. Her first real hit.

"Flora," I heard Mum calling from the stairs, "what do you want to do for dinner tonight?"

My heart dropped. Bugger. She was going to find these and think I'd done this. Crap. Oh crap, crap, crap.

"I was thinking about something chicken-y, but I haven't decided."

She was at my bedroom door before I could do anything. My feet were rooted to the spot as I held the innards from her proudest achievement. Her eyes met mine, looked a bit muddled, and then fell to the objects in my hands.

Now the realisation wave hit her. Although it seemed to hit her ten times faster than it had hit me.

"I can't believe you'd do this," she said. "And when did you do this? Was it when we'd had the fight? Or was it the "*This place is a murder house*" day?"

"Mum." I tried to persuade her to believe me. "I literally just found these in my cupboard. I didn't even know they were from your book until you just walked in here."

"I don't understand you, Flora," she said with a horribly disappointed shake of her head. "We went out and had a nice day, and now you throw it in my face."

"No," I said, "I'm not throwing anything. "I honestly just found this. And I wouldn't—"

"Look, I know that you're angry and lonely here," she said, more reasonably than I was expecting. "But I am too. And I need you to give this a chance." Tears pressed at my eyes as she continued, "I need to make it work here. We both do. I need you to grow up and act like you give a damn about someone other than yourself."

She stepped forward and snatched the papers from my hands.

"I'm sorry," I whispered. Not for the pages, but for everything.

Mum said nothing and left. She shut the door behind her. I was trembling and I glanced around the room. Miles did this.

I had wanted to give him the benefit of the doubt. I thought he was a sad, lonely guy who had needed help. But this wasn't someone who was asking for help. This was someone who was asking for attention.

There was a creak near the cupboard. Someone was watching our fight. Goosebumps spread over my arms.

"Get out," I whispered with my teeth gritted.

There was a moment of quiet, and then, the unthinkable happened—my bedroom door clicked open and then shut again. My heart pounded as I stood alone in my room. I could only hope and pray that he actually had left.

This wasn't a poor, lonely boy. Miles was a stalker, and he was making sure I knew it.

Him

I don't leave because she tells me to, I leave because I want to follow her stupid mother. Opening and closing the door is for Flora's benefit, letting her know that I'm doing as she's asked.

She must know by now that I can come and go as I please. I don't need doors.

I follow her mother, who storms down to her library. She's already crying before she's even halfway there. Once inside, she slams the door behind her and presses the torn pages to her chest. I'm already inside, stepping through the wall without any trouble. Sobs heave out of her, but she tries to stay quiet. She goes to the bookcase and picks up the book the pages have come from. My damage is clear. Pages are bent, torn, and covered with dust and dirt. She presses the pages back where they belong and puts the book back on the shelf. I watch as she takes her glasses off and wipes at her eyes.

She's broken and thinks that Flora has betrayed her. I wonder if my mother ever looked like this after one of our fights.

Her mother threw all my stuff out. She thinks this will stop me. I did not spend years in a box to be moved to a bin, and now, she knows that.

I'm learning new tricks. It's easier with all of the things that were locked away with me. They were easy enough to retrieve and put together. I feel myself growing stronger every day. Her mother can see that now.

I wrote to Flora today. She threw it under the bed and called it shit.

She will see me, too. She will see how strong I am becoming.

Then we'll see who's shit.

Chapter Eight

Flora

I woke up to my phone vibrating with a message. Waking today felt like waking with an emotional hangover after the incident with Mum. It all rushed back to me, and I felt awful.

The phone buzzed with a second message. For some reason, I convinced myself it was from Dad and jumped up with excitement to answer it. It wasn't Dad—of course it wasn't. Instead, it was a number I didn't recognise. I opened it and was greeted with a pleasant surprise.

Hey. My mum gave me your number and insisted that I tell you that "library clubs are a wonderful social experience," but instead I just thought I'd ask if you've got any good Archival theories. I use the Cycle forums, if you wanna add me as a friend on that. My ID is RhythmIsADancer. Totally cool if you don't.

Underneath, the second message read:

This is Charlie, by the way.

Even though I was disappointed that it wasn't Dad—and peeved that Charlie was messaging at 8:30 on a Sunday morning—I suddenly felt sort of excited. Before even responding, I jumped out of bed and fired up my PC. I logged on and then I waited.

Having a romance-writing mother means that I had been subjected to every magazine, TV, and online interview she has ever done. During these interviews, she was always asked to give out relationship advice. Some of it had inadvertently seeped into my malleable teenage brain. So, I decided not to text back straight away so as not to seem desperate. The part of my brain that rejected this relationship advice thought I was being stupid, and that I should just message him ASAP.

I fired up the *Archival Cycle* fan forum and typed his username into the search bar. I hovered the mouse over the "*Add Friend*" button, but I did not click.

Patience, Flora, I urged myself. *Did the Rangers fire when Ophie broke into the Guild at the end of Book Two, or did they wait for the right moment? Guess I'll wait then.*

So, I went for a shower and got changed first.

Smooth, Flora, super smooth. Like butter. Or something sexier. Like maple syrup. Maybe something less sticky. Who knows?

Granted, this was the fastest shower, hair drying, and clothes changing in the history of man. Whizzing downstairs, I flicked on the kettle and made tea for both Mum and me and whipped up some Pop-Tarts. Just as I was adding the milk to the tea, Mum appeared in her pyjamas.

"What's happening here?" she asked, putting on her glasses as if she couldn't believe what she was seeing.

"You made breakfast yesterday, so I thought I'd do it today," I said as if it was the most natural thing ever. I was trying incredibly hard not to say, "*Sorry a ghost possibly ripped up one of your books*".

"Pop-Tarts?" Mum said, eyeing the toaster carefully. There was an awkwardness in the air, and we could both feel it.

"For me, yeah. You've got toast and honey and banana," I replied, pointing at the table. Sure enough, there was a plate of fresh toast, banana and honey, and a tea in her guilty pleasure *True Blood* mug. I, on the other hand, had mine in a *Wall-E* mug (the greatest Pixar film of all time—fight me if you think I'm wrong). "And I know this can't possibly make up for everything, but I've ordered you a new copy of Ravensdale. I maintain my innocence on the pages, but I was guilty of the general angst and shittiness."

I gave her a kiss on the cheek and rushed upstairs with my breakfast before she had the chance to question me any further on the book or keep from the potential for Charlie chat.

Now was time to send the friend request. I hit send and grabbed my phone. First, I saved his number to my contacts. Charlie sat beside a collection of Glaswegian contacts who I had no idea if I'd ever see again. This morning, I didn't even care. For just now, he was the only contact that mattered.

Next, it was time to construct a clever response.

Hey Charlie. So nice to hear from you. It was nice to meet you yesterday.

That was stupid. I technically met him last week. Plus, it sounded like the kind of message my mum would send, and using the word "nice" twice was lazy. Delete.

Charlie! Thanks so much. I would love to join the library stuff and I'd love some book chat.

That's a lot of love for someone I barely knew. Delete.

Rather than try to come up with something clever, I went for a meme. I found one of the characters on his t-shirt with the caption *"Let's do this"* and hit send.

Almost simultaneously, my friend request was accepted, and he replied to my message with a laughing emoji. Taking a quick drink of tea and a bite of a Pop-Tart, I accepted his invite to a private chat. As the connection kicked in, his avatar popped up in the chatbox. It was a hand-drawn picture of Freiten—the love interest in Book Two who is killed at the very beginning of Book Three. Spoilers, sorry.

Your username is QueenOfTheDamned? he messaged before he even said hello.

I happen to love Anne Rice, I defended. *You've got a cheek to talk, RhythmIsADancer.*

Hey, in my house, if you don't dance, you don't eat.

That doesn't sound even remotely true.

He sent a GIF of a dancing puppy. I responded with a laughing GIF.

We went through the usual kind of forum chat. What book is your favourite? Which Guild would you belong to? Who's your favourite character and why is it not Babs, the anthropomorphic coat?

I did everything I could to avoid talking about the TV show. I thought it would ruin things if he knew my dad was involved with making it. Also, I didn't want to answer why I wasn't getting daily updates from the set. That would be kind of awkward, especially considering I couldn't actually answer that question.

Several hours flew by before we knew it and he had to leave to help his mum with something. It was the fastest morning I'd spent in this stupid village. It also helped that we hadn't actually talked about anything personal—it had all been book chat. That made everything easier.

See you in English tomorrow? Charlie asked as I prepared to log off.

Sure thing, I agreed. *History, too?*

Damn, I totally forgot about history. He added a sad emoji. *I'm so behind.*

Join the club. I giggled, adding a laughing emoji.

Speaking of, he added, *I'm contractually obliged by Mrs. Newman, both our mothers, and the rest of the writing and/or book group to formally invite you to come along after school tomorrow. You in?*

I think I'm in, I said.

Damn right you are, he typed.

I felt as if I could see him smiling through the words. He probably wasn't. I was pretty sure that I was daydreaming.

We both logged off, and I spent the rest of the day grinning. Well, that and quickly pulling together a short story so that I had something to read at this bloody writing group. It was some sickly sweet sci-fi, but it was what I was in the mood for.

Sometimes sickly sweet is just sweet enough.

Before I went to bed, I gave it a quick reread to make sure that I was happy enough with what I'd managed to throw together. It wasn't my best work, but it was something harmless that was acceptable enough for a writing group. A little sci-fi slice of life story about a boy getting his first little spaceship and his girlfriend being too scared to take a ride in it. Cute.

It wasn't going to win any awards, but it seemed like an acceptable start to something silly that might wind up turning into something cool. In my head, I pictured it morphing into a rip-roaring adventure in space. Maybe there was something in the cargo hold that led them to great riches? Maybe there was someone following them, and the previous owner had been a spy? Or maybe, they just took a wrong turn and spent the rest of the story searching the galaxy for a way back home.

It didn't matter. What mattered was that I wasn't going in empty-handed. I was prepared and I had some cool people to meet. Some people like Charlie.

I put my notepad on the bedside table with my pen still tucked into the page where my story was written, just in case I woke up during the night with a better idea or a way to improve this story a bit. It wouldn't have been my first session of midnight writing. However, I soon found myself asleep. I didn't stir until morning, leaving no time to write the master-piece I dreamt of.

Him

This morning I've been sitting on the edge of her bed, watching her exchange messages back and forth with someone called Charlie. Eventually, I wind up standing at her back, leaning over her shoulder so I can read it all.

Even though she's ruining everything by talking to another man, she looks really beautiful today. It's hard to be mad at her when she looks this good. She's wearing lots of layers against the cold February morning. A long, knitted cardigan stretches over her behind and skirts where her dark grey leggings cling to her thighs. It's a mauve colour, and it sits on top of a loose-fitting top with a delicate skull print on it.

On at least three occasions, she swipes her hand in my direction as if swiping away a fly or an unwelcome draft. I do not move away. I move closer. I stare at her. This was the closest I'd dared to get to her. She smells like honey. I want to taste her.

Hovering my hand over her hair, I imagine running my fingers through it. Dark waves call to me and beg to be touched. It hugs her neck and drifts over her chest. I look down and her top is hanging forward. The glimpse of her bra would have made my heart quicken if it was still beating.

She laughs at something this Charlie creature says. It breaks the spell, and I stagger backwards as if she'd slapped me in the face. Drifting onto the bed, I lie here for the rest of the day. She moves around me like she's the ghost. Picking things up. Messaging this boy. Listening to music. Never once looking my way.

At some point in the afternoon, she takes up residence in the bed with me and starts scrawling in her notepad. I turn on my side and watch her work. Her eyes dart over the text, rereading sections after she writes them. Her teeth gently rest on the tip of her pen as she thinks. Her brow furrows as she scores out a word and replaces it with one that she deems better.

It takes her hours. It never ever took me that long to write a poem. My words flowed like blood from a ruptured vein, pumping and pumping until my life was on the page, and I certainly didn't change things when I was done. That would be like deciding I wasn't good enough. My poems had to be raw.

Now it's night, and she's left the notepad sitting on her bedside table. When I know she's asleep, I muster up all the strength I have and reach for the book and the pen. I lift it and it feels like ten hardback books strapped together. Certainly not a light

*notebook with some forest illustration on the cardboard cover.
I'm getting better at this but it's so, so hard.*

*I read the words she had written. False hope, lies, and clear
Disneyfication stain the page. It's disgusting.*

And she'd called my writing shit?

Chapter Nine

Flora

My alarm went off bright and early, and I woke up with a bounce. Competing with yesterday's record-setting getting-ready time, I showered, dressed, did a tiny bit of makeup, and packed my bag a full half-hour earlier than I normally do. I packed my notepad swiftly, not bothering to reread it. Mostly, this was out of fear that I'd decide it was rubbish, rip it out, and conclude that I shouldn't go. I was prone to strops like that, so I was determined not to let myself fall victim to one today. I was fighting my "inner saboteur," as my mum used to call it before she pretty much became an outer saboteur and stopped doing anything creative at all.

Taking the stairs two at a time, I practically bounded into the kitchen. It seemed I had beaten Mum to being first up again. Today felt like a porridge day, and I had time to spare. I made a pot, along with two cups of tea. My porridge was doused in maple syrup, while Mum's was left in the pot for when she woke up. It was a little weird that she wasn't awake yet, but I decided to leave her to it. I left a note, stating that there was porridge in the pot, tea on the counter, and that I'd be late in tonight because I had given in to peer pressure and would be attending the writing group after school. I dropped my bowl in the sink and turned the hob off, making sure that I didn't kill Mum with porridge-flavoured good intentions. She'd just have to eat it cold.

I headed out into the grey morning and wished the school day away, praying for half-past three to come sooner.

Charlie waited for me after fourth period English class.

"Hey there, QueenoftheDamned," he said.

"Well hello, RhythmIsADancer," I said right back. "How are you today?"

"I'm excellent," he smiled. "Just about to head home for lunch. What about you?"

"I'm actually still laughing that you thought the character Hirophel was pronounced "high-ro-fell" and not "hee-ro-fel" like the rest of us normal people."

"You should never make fun of a person for mispronouncing a word because it means they've learned it from reading it in a book," he said with his finger raised as it to emphasise his point. "Or so I've heard."

"I think that counts for vocabulary and not the names of fantasy characters," I said.

"Who cares? She dies in Book One."

"Said like a true Hirophel fan."

"Very funny, but I have to run—I'm far too busy and important for the likes of you," he said with a wink. "Catch you later?" he added, his voice a little softer.

"Absolutely. Go enjoy your lunch." I smiled, watching him walk away. Maybe I actually could make friends in this place. This buoyed me for the rest of the day as the afternoon flew by.

After last period, I gathered up my things as quickly as I could and headed for the library. I was pretty sure that I would be the first there and this would probably make me look a little sad (I remembered Mum's ridiculous relationship advice: never be on time for a date—it reeks of desperation. Make him wait for you), but I didn't even remotely care. I just wanted to get there.

Luckily, Lydia the Goth was lurking at my locker when I stopped by to pick up my notepad. It was the first time I'd actually been glad to see her. She smiled past her dark lipstick and pressed a leather-bound journal to her chest.

"Hey, new girl," she said to me, tapping long, silver nails against the cover of her book. "I heard you met my stupid brother."

"I did, indeed," I said, shutting my locker over. "And I heard you're also in the writers' group."

"I'm the next Lovecraft," she purred. "But without all the racism. And the sexism. Actually, just the tentacles, really."

"That sounds...excellent."

"It's not."

"No?"

"Everybody hates it." Lydia said, her voice entirely deadpan and matter-of-fact.

"I'm sorry."

"It's fine. I think I'm meant to be misunderstood in my own time. Future freaks will love it."

"That's very optimistic," I commended. "I like it."

We started to walk to the library. She was wearing a long swishy skirt, and I could see Doc Martins poking out from underneath. Tiny stars and moons had been drawn on the dark leather with a silver pen. They actually looked kind of cool. I felt rotten for all the sassy comments I've said about her to Mum over the last week.

"So, Charlie says you're an *Archivist*?" She smiled.

"Very much so."

"That's good. You know, those books mean a lot to him and me. We read them together just after our dad died."

I felt winded by this information she'd just thrown at me. I had no idea. Charlie hadn't said anything, and neither had his mum. Well, I guess it's not something you toss around, is it? *"Oh hi, I'm Sara, and I'm a widow."*

"Oh. I didn't know. I'm sorry." I said, totally shocked.

"It's fine. He was a dick anyway," Lydia muttered. "The books are cool, though."

My head was going faster than my mouth was, and I couldn't pull a response out in time before she was at the library door.

Her smile was back, having only briefly slipped. "I hope you brought something other than crappy poems because I swear to god if I have to read one more poem about the perils of puberty or someone's dead granny, I might scream."

"No poems here," I told her honestly.

When she grinned, her lower lip piercing danced up and down. I couldn't stop thinking the words "dead dad," but I said nothing and instead tried to steel myself for what was to come.

Taking a deep breath, I pulled the library door open, ready to put my literary heart on my sleeve and see what everyone thought. It turned out I was not the first one there. Two girls had beaten me to it. One was frantically writing in a journal adorned with ribbons, and the other was sat on the desk that the other one wrote on. Surely that was inconvenient, but the one who was writing didn't seem to mind. The one who was on the desk looked up as I entered. She had long, wavy fair hair and dark eyes that didn't seem to match her pale locks. Heavy boots hung from her feet as they dangled from the desk. She eyed me carefully, as if I had walked in by mistake.

"Nadia, please," said a voice that I recognised. "Get off the desk." Mrs. Newman appeared with a cup of tea in her hand. It was an entirely different mug from the one I had seen her with the other day—how many did she have back there? "Flora!" she gushed as she turned around to see me standing at the door.

"Sorry Miss," the girl named Nadia mumbled as she hopped down and grabbed a seat next to the writing girl. Her gaze stayed on me the entire time.

Mrs. Newman pulled me over to the table, taking me gently by the arm. "Oh, Flora, I'm so happy you decided to join us." She beamed. "This is Nadia, and this is Lisa—two of our most enthusiastic members! And I see you've already met our 'Queen of Horror,' Lydia."

"We're going with 'Queen of the Obscene' now, Miss," Lydia informed her, sitting down beside Nadia and giving her a nod before whipping her phone out. The leather notebook lay on the table, tempting me with wanting to see what was in it.

The other girl didn't seem interested in Lydia at all, but she was more than happy to see me. Lisa, the writer, lifted her head to reveal a face full of bright freckles. She smiled widely in a way that revealed a mouthful of white teeth. Her red hair was pulled back in a messy plait, and she spoke in the most northern accent I'd heard the entire time I'd lived here.

"Hi Flora!" she giggled. "Don't mind me, I'm just finishing something. I had an idea last class, and if I don't write it down now, I'll forget it. I've got a head like a sieve!"

A chair slid out on the opposite side of the table, allowing me to sit down; it took me a moment to realise that it was Nadia pushing it with her foot. She stared at me and then nodded to the seat. Obediently, I sat down, pressing my bag into my lap. As I sat down, Mrs. Newman realised she had forgotten something and rushed off to her office to get it. I was left alone with two strangers and Lydia, the strangest of all.

"You awright?" Nadia asked me, finally speaking her first words since I'd sat down.

"Yeah, I guess so," I responded, a little bit afraid. "You?"

"Yeah." She nodded. "I heard you're from Glasgow. Have you ever seen someone get stabbed?"

I snorted until I realised she was being serious. "Erm...no. No stabbings here."

"Shame."

Lisa quickly finished what she was writing and closed her notepad with a flourish. "Done!" she said, turning to Nadia with a smile.

Nadia attempted to smile back, but it was more like a grimace. "Good job," she said with a shrug.

"Well, Flora, you must be just as bored as the rest of us here if you're joining a school club after just a week," Lisa said, turning her attention back to me, giving me a wink that said she was only kidding.

"Definitely," I agreed. "Bored out my face."

"Thought as much," she said with another giggle. She was pretty damn delightful. I struggled to find the urge, which I'd had last week when I was in the library to flee here.

Nadia, however, continued to stare. "Are you the Psycho House Feminazi?" she asked.

Lisa gasped and kicked Nadia under the table. "Oh my God, Nads, you can't just ask people if they're the Psycho House Feminazi!"

"Well, are you?" Nadia asked again, ignoring Lisa entirely.

"I guess so," I sighed.

"Good." Nadia nodded and reached her hand across the table. Tentatively, I took it. She shook it hard in an enthusiastic way, as if she had just made the business deal of a lifetime. "You can stay. You and I are going to be good friends."

I chuckled and felt all of the pent-up air I'd been holding in my chest come rushing out.

"Now hurry up and take your Twitter off private so I can see what's got Phil the Prick so fired up," she added, and a smirk appeared at the corner of her lips. "I hate that guy."

"Sure." I nodded. I quietly chastised myself for giving in to a bully and making my account private in the first place.

The library doors opened, and two boys entered. One was Charlie. The other was in a fairly tidy uniform, contrasting with Charlie's skater style. Boy number two had a well-done tie and a straightened blazer. His hair was slicked back away from his face, and he had a soft smile. Charlie was laughing with his mouth wide open. I wanted to share his laughter. He lifted his head, and our eyes met.

Sparks, fireworks, so many clichés.

I think I liked this boy.

Lydia cleared her throat, and I pulled my eyes back to her. She cocked an eyebrow and gave me a smirk. The fireworks dissolved with a quiet fizzle.

Charlie pulled up the seat next to me, and his companion joined him. Nadia gave him a gruff nod and a wink. Lisa reached over to the other boy and grabbed his arm, yanking his sleeve up and taking a pen to his flesh.

"Eh, excuse me?!" the boy demanded. "What are you playing at, Lisa?"

She didn't respond and finished writing a name on his arm. It read "Night Bus by Gabrielle Aplin." She said, "I found this lassie on YouTube last week, and it was exactly like that thing you read a couple of weeks ago. I wanted you to listen to it."

"Could you not just send me the link?" the boy asked, looking at the neatly written song and artist on his forearm.

"I forgot." She shrugged and leaned back in her chair.

Charlie gave me a smile. "Hey."

"Hey," I said back.

"This is Tom," he said, gesturing a thumb in Tom's direction. He swung around to catch the eye of Tom, who was now attempting to rub away the words "Night Bus" from his arm. "Tom, this is Flora."

Tom gave me a little wave. "Is he who talked you into coming along to this, then?" he asked me, after giving up and pulling his sleeve back down.

"It was a coordinated strike," I said, pointing at Mrs. Newman's office and then back at Charlie.

"Buggers." Tom shook his head. "Another good soldier conscripted into this unruly troop."

"Precisely," I agreed.

"You're acting like you don't consider yourself the commander," Charlie said to his friend.

"I think we all know that's Lydia's position," Lisa chimed in.

Lydia grinned and stretched out her arms, fingers extended and wiggling, as if summoning all the demons of Hell. Her glasses took up a large amount of space on her face and somehow seemed to compliment her dark lipstick, which I'm almost sure she probably hadn't worn to class all day.

"What's up, witches?" She grinned from her seat at the head of the table.

Oh yes, this girl was certainly in charge.

The rest of the group gravitated towards her, and I imagined the room lights dimming and a single spotlight landing on her. She was the star of the show. Everyone started to talk, animated to the point that I could barely focus on what any one person was saying. Instead, I just kept watching Lydia as if she were made of magic. White teeth bit her painted lip, and her painted nails toyed with the rim of her hat. When she eventually took the hat off, a wave of dark hair danced over her shoulders.

"Let's all be nice to Flora, shall we?" she announced once she had finished fluffing her hair. "She's the most exciting thing to happen to this school in years. I was getting fed-up of these Plain Janes."

Nadia casually raised a middle finger in Lydia's direction.

"You coming to book club as well?" Lydia asked me.

"I haven't really decided yet," I said.

"Oh, you definitely should," she breezed. "There's more readers anyway, so it isn't just us. There's a bunch of other kids, so you'll probably feel a little less exposed."

"That sounds good," I said, feeling relieved already.

"Remind me to help you find a copy of the book when we're done here. It's not the *Archival Cycle*, but it's okay so far."

"I will," I agreed.

Before I could agree to anything else, Mrs. Newman returned with a full cup of tea and pulled up another seat. The group went over some points from their last meeting. Obviously, I couldn't contribute to this at all, but it was still exciting to listen to. They discussed a competition Mrs. Newman had found that was nearing the deadline. It seemed that Lisa had been working on something and Lydia had been proofreading for her. Mrs. Newman stressed how important meeting deadlines was, and that this was a great opportunity. Then, they went on to discuss some of the website stuff, and Charlie took over. One of Tom's pieces had been getting a lot of hits, and Charlie was trying to get a piece from everyone while there was traffic coming their way. Everyone agreed apart from Nadia. She said that this was not "her chosen outlet", and she hands-down did not want to have her work online. Everyone groaned, as if this was a speech they had heard repeatedly.

There was something really nice about listening to everybody jumping in and out of the discussion—they were a thriving, active community intent on sharing ideas. It made the photographs in the old yearbook suddenly three-dimensional. When I'd first stepped into this library, that was all I'd seen it as. A photograph. Now, it seemed so full of life. For the first time since I'd arrived here, I started to feel like I could maybe even belong here.

Mrs. Newman very briefly introduced me. She just said that my name was Flora and I'd moved here from Glasgow. I deeply appreciated the fact that she didn't mention that my mum was a writer. Instead, she reminded me that I didn't have to share anything since it was my first session, but that I was welcome to if I wanted to.

I admitted to the group that I actually did have something, but that I probably wouldn't go first if that was okay. Everyone totally agreed and seemed pleased that I wanted to share anything at all. I began to feel warm and fuzzy inside in a way that was truly cringe-worthy and disgusting. But who cared?

Nadia volunteered to go first and went into her large burlap tote bag, stencilled with an image of Frida Kahlo. Half a dozen paper booklets were pulled out and handed around the table. What I held in front of me looked like it was straight out of a time machine. It was a photocopied zine. My face lit up as I started to flick through it—lyrics to Bikini Kill songs, pictures of Hedy Lamarr, and a Dorothy Parker poem. On the back was an article from the *Geena Davis Institute on Gender in the Media* about the percentage of talking roles in films last year that were taken up by women (not enough, it concluded). All of it was framed with highlighter pens.

"Now, Nadia," Mrs Newman began, "I was hoping that you might actually write something yourself this week."

"Well," Nadia countered, "this is a creative writing group, and I'm using it to creatively distribute writing."

"Other people's writing," Mrs. Newman corrected.

"I do not see anything wrong with that," Nadia answered.

"Me neither," I replied, trying not to be too controversial on my first visit but thinking I shouldn't shy away from what I thought. "There's a lot of work in this," I said, flicking open to a page where an annotated poem was displayed. "And I think it's a really creative medium. Maybe we could all contribute something to another one?" I asked Nadia, whose face was filled with sheer joy.

Mrs. Newman cleared her throat. "As someone who has seen some of Nadia's more...inflammatory... zines, it may be best if we *all* curate any intended for distribution in school."

"You can come back," Nadia told me before sitting back down. She let me keep my copy of her zine. The rest were swiped back and pushed into her bag—photocopying wasn't cheap, you know.

Tom stood up next and read out a very poignant and poetic story where a man walked down a lamplit street in a park. Nothing happened, and he didn't actually go anywhere. No conclusions were reached, and some of the language was overly stylistic. However, everyone seemed to like it. Tom sat down again, looking pleased with himself.

Lisa passed, deciding that she'd discovered a huge plot hole in the piece she'd been frantically scribbling when I arrived. For the rest of the session, she continued to write. Nobody seemed to mind this and left her to it.

Then it came to me. I fished my notebook out of my bag and stood up. I realised that nobody else had stood up when they read and hovered over my seat as I tried to decide what to do. As I opened the book and flicked my way through, I scanned the expectant faces around me. Maybe this wasn't such a good idea. Or maybe, I should stop being a worrier and get on with it. My bum hit the seat again and I decided I'd do this sitting down.

Then I realised that I couldn't find the piece I'd written the night before. I had actually written it, right? Panic started to rise, and my brow furrowed as I searched the book. My fingers hit something hideous. A rip in the centre of the book, indicating that pages had been removed. I ran my fingers over the jagged tear, evidence of something horrible.

"Everything okay?" Mrs. Newman asked. I looked up to see that the expectant faces had all slightly morphed into something that was tinted with confusion.

I opened the back page and discovered a folded piece of paper. Slowly, I unfolded it to find something I didn't remember writing. My eyes skimmed it and searched for my story. It was gone. My stomach felt like it was about to fall through the floor as I read what was there instead. It wasn't my handwriting.

The note said: "I thought you were supposed to be a writer?" in a dark scrawl.

"I'm really sorry," I said quietly. "I think I've lifted the wrong book."

"Oh, that's perfectly fine," Mrs. Newman said with a kind face. I glanced around and saw at least two faces that didn't believe me. They probably thought that I was just nervous and didn't want to read aloud. Awkwardly, I sat back down and looked at the folded piece of paper. I didn't write this.

"You okay?" Charlie whispered.

I nodded and tried not to cry.

Meanwhile, Lydia stood up. She didn't hesitate as she got to her feet and gave me a wink, signalling that I was okay. Saving the best for last, she read out a beautifully gothic piece that I could barely listen to. Instead, I quickly reread the note that had harboured passage in my notepad.

I tried to focus on Lydia's story. Everyone seemed to love it and had plenty to say about it. I kept my mouth shut. The words from the note in my book swirled in my head.

The group came to an end, and everyone began to disperse. Tom was the first away, followed by Lisa and Nadia. I was left with Lydia and Charlie. Lydia thanked me for coming and then vanished to find a copy of the book club reading. It was a tad alarming that she was talking like it was her club, but it wasn't my place to say, so I let it go.

"That was some excellent reading you did there," Charlie joked. I tried not to look hurt, but I must have still been a little teary-eyed. "Oh no, I'm sorry. Humour is my default setting."

"No," I said, giving my eyes a quick wipe. "It's my own fault. I did write something yesterday, but I didn't check what I lifted this morning. I'm so stupid."

"Happens to the best of us," Charlie said, giving me an attempt at a reassuring smile. "And you're not stupid."

"Whatever," I grumbled.

The quietness returned and this time it was awkward.

"You've got a long walk home, right?" he asked, breaking the silence.

"Yeah."

"I could walk you some of the way if you'd like," he offered.

"*We* could walk you," Lydia interrupted, sweeping back in and pressing the book club book into my hands. It was a narrative poem about a young Black drag queen. It looked really cool. "Back off Charlie, she's mine."

"Oh no, I couldn't make you do that," I said.

Charlie ignored his sister. "Nah, it wouldn't put us out or anything. Anyway, you'd be saving me from Mum's salsa night. I can't face being her "volunteer" again when nobody offers to demonstrate the steps," he joked. Humour really was his default setting.

"I'll be fine," I replied, laughing at the thought of him salsa dancing. Plus, by this point, I just wanted to get home and curl up in a ball.

Eventually, he caved, and we waved each other off.

Lydia grabbed my arm as we passed our lockers, letting Charlie walk ahead. "I know that I joked with Charlie to "back off, you're mine", but not like that. I have a girlfriend. You wouldn't know her—she goes to school in Inverness..."

She said all of this nearly in one breath, and sometimes I worried that talking like this must be exhausting for her.

She continued, "I mean it. It's cool to meet someone who everyone else thinks is a weirdo, but I really do think we might wind up being pals."

"What about all those people in there?" I asked. "Aren't they your mates?"

"Eugh. Right, Nadia has good intentions, but is just happy that people will listen to her. Lisa is a child genius and only wants to talk about things that will win her prizes. Tom is part of Phil's gang and is honestly just here so he can put something on his UCAS form. So, it's great to finally have someone new who's here to talk stories and spooky stuff."

Her bravado slipped, and I saw someone really forlorn.

"Nobody here really gave a damn about Charlie and me when bad stuff happened. We just became those kids whose dad died. I drag Charlie to all this stuff so he doesn't just clock in and out of school. He's got skater pals he sees at the weekend, but he would literally talk to nobody here if I didn't push him."

"That sounds tough." I nodded.

"I know that people have been dicks to you already here, but you don't have to go solo on that. Us weird gals gotta stick together."

I laughed. "How have I wound up as one of the weird gals already?"

"You live in a murder house." She shrugged and pulled her dramatic hat back on.

As if mirroring Lydia, my guard began to drop and before I could stop myself, I said something stupid. "You know the really weird thing? I did have a story in that notebook, and somebody ripped it out."

I let the book fall open to reveal the tear. Lydia was suddenly super interested and grabbed it off me. The folded bit of paper fell from the pages like a dead leaf.

"And that was there instead," I added as she scooped it up. I gestured to the note.

"What the hell?" Lydia muttered as she read it. I tried not to look scared, but I think I was doing a terrible job. A beat of silence followed as Lydia tried to decide whether to believe me or not and I wished that she would.

"Tell you what," she said. "I'm totally keeping this as a prompt for next week's writers' group. That cool with you?"

I nodded and was relieved to have it taken off my hands. Lydia gave me a wink and tucked the piece of phantom writing in her pocket, and we said goodnight.

I began the trudge home in the light rain. At this time of night, it was dark, and I couldn't see the puddles before I jammed my foot in them. What had started off as a great day had ended up a bit soggy after all.

By the time I got home, Mum was nowhere to be found. When I went into the kitchen to make myself a sad and lonely Pot Noodle, I saw this morning's breakfast congealed in the pot. I ran it under the tap and filled it with soapy water to soak. Her teacup was still sitting, with a layer of clotted old milk lying on top. I instantly knew what had happened.

I went upstairs and pushed Mum's room door open. An episode of *Friends* was playing on the TV she had in her bedroom, but she was paying no attention to it. She was still in her pyjamas, and the bed was littered with tissues. Empty crisp packets lay on a messy circle around the bed like they had been placed there for some kind of slovenly ritual to take place.

When I walked in, she was in the middle of blowing her nose. "Oh, hi sweetie," she tried to say as if nothing was wrong. I knew exactly what had happened.

"I take it Dad phoned," I said, as I sat on the corner of the bed.

She nodded. "Yesterday," she replied, chucking the hankie she had just used onto the bundle that was forming at the foot of the bed, not far from where I sat.

"Yesterday?" My sympathy for her (which I convince myself I won't have every time she goes through one of these, yet here I was) dwindled and was replaced with a feeling of betrayal. "Why didn't you let me talk to him?"

"I heard you talking on your computer with your friend and didn't want to ruin the fun you were having."

"Ruin my fun?" I was starting to get angry. "You didn't tell me Dad was on the phone because I was chatting with someone I barely know?!"

"Flora, please..."

"No way, Mum." Heat travelled in hot lines up my face, bursting into light on my cheekbones. "You can't do this. You can't dump Dad and then expect me to hate him because you do. You dumped him, Mum. The divorce was your—"

"He wanted me to tell you about her," she said. All of a sudden, she was very calm. The ripples of sadness and distress were still there, but she was downright refusing to rise to my temper. "The woman your dad was having an affair with," Mum said as simply as she could.

"What?"

"They met on that stupid detective show your dad worked on for the BBC. She's a make-up artist." At this, my mum rolled her eyes. I wanted to call her out on being judgemental over stupid things, but this really wasn't the time. "When he went down to London, he took her with him."

I hadn't noticed that I'd been shaking my head the whole time. News like this wasn't for hearing on a tissue-covered bed while "The One with the Chandler in a Box" was playing in the background. The canned laughter seemed to be laughing at us, not Matthew Perry and Matt LeBlanc.

"I'm sorry, sweetie," Mum said, reaching for another tissue. This one was for me, not her.

"Did he ask to speak to me?" I asked naively.

Mum shook her head. "He wanted me to tell you who she was. It would seem that things are getting serious."

"I don't want to meet her," I spat out.

"You don't have to," Mum said. "Not unless you want to." She held out an arm, and I took it. Folding me in against her, we both cried in a way that neither of us had since we'd sold the Glasgow house. She buried her face in my hair as I hid in her chest. I don't know how long we spent like that. Long enough for me to realise I was still in my school uniform. I went to change into pyjamas and joined Mum in bed. We fell asleep after about seven more episodes of *Friends*.

I never got around to eating my Pot Noodle.

Him

She has done nothing about my note. I did her a favour by trashing that worthless drivel she wrote, and she hasn't even thanked me. Think of the embarrassment she would have faced in front of those idiots from school. I saved her from that.

Despite this, she doesn't even seem to care.

Her mother has been crying in bed all day—just like my own useless parents. They did nothing. If they were ever in the house, they certainly didn't give a shit about me. Instead, my father was parked in front of the TV, and my mother was crying over the ironing.

Useless.

I'm watching Flora and that lazy mother of hers right now from the door to her mother's bedroom. They're watching crap sitcoms and laughing when the audio cues tell them to. I try to get Flora's attention. I've been tapping on the bedroom door, but they have the volume on the TV up too high. I want to bang on it. I want to punch a fucking hole through it.

I'm angry and sad for her, but I'm also angry and sad for me. I just want her to see me.

Why won't she see me?

Eventually, they both fall asleep, and I want to try something. I stand over Flora and try to command her to stand. I whisper and I hiss and I yell and I scream. Eyes remain closed but her head lifts. I feel a smile stretching on my broken face.

This is going to be excellent.

Chapter Ten

Flora

Mum let me sleep in a little. I had horrible dreams about the lake outside the house last night. I imagined standing at the edge of it and leaning over to look at the water. From below the surface, Miles' face looked out at me. The whole time, he screamed wildly.

Breakfast was served in Mum's bed, and after, she offered to drive me to school. I didn't bother fighting it today. I didn't care what people thought if the new girl's mum gave her a lift. When I stood up, my feet landed in a puddle of mud on Mum's bedroom floor. Maybe I'd forgotten to take my boots off downstairs yesterday? Now, my feet were filthy. Great.

Things only got weirder when I searched Mum's room for my boots, only to find them downstairs, sitting by the front door, where I usually left them. A strange flicker of a dream came back to me. Something about me standing outside at the lake on the way up to the house. Glancing down at my dirty feet, I shook my head. Surely, I hadn't been sleepwalking. It was just a nightmare—definitely just a nightmare. I put it down to a poor sleep and broken dreams and climbed into the car with Mum.

We said nothing in the car, and she played some of my music. However, we couldn't listen to very much of it; it wasn't a very long drive.

As I got out of the car, Mum reached over and took my hand. "You and me, sweetie," she said with the kind of nod like she'd inwardly decided on something important.

"You and me, Mum," I said, and got out of the car.

I caught a look of myself in the car window and realised that I looked a right state. I hadn't washed my hair, which was scraped back into a messy ponytail, strands sticking out all over the place. I had lazily pulled yesterday's uniform back on and pulled fresh knickers and socks out of the dryer. In fact, I hadn't been in my room for more than a couple of minutes over the last twenty-four hours. This meant that I was missing a couple of necessary textbooks, but I could play the new girl card and borrow from teachers throughout the day.

At lunch, I stepped into the cafeteria, prepared to do my usual – eat as quickly as possible then go hide somewhere and read – but Lydia spotted me immediately. No hat was worn today so she was a little trickier to spot. She waved me over to a table where she sat with Nadia and Lisa. They seemed pleased to see me, despite my lack of reading the previous night and my current physical state.

Lisa was reading the book club book, with her legs stretched across Nadia's lap, using her as a human footstool. Nadia didn't seem to mind and was eating some kind of veggie wrap. Lydia ushered me into the seat next to her and proceeded to bombard me with questions.

"How'd you find writers' group, then?" she started with.

"Pretty good," I said honestly. "You seem a very talented bunch."

"Lies!" Lisa chimed in from over her book. She immediately went back to reading and acted like she wasn't listening.

"I'm sorry that your notepad didn't have what you were looking for," Lydia continued, eying me from over her statement glasses. It was clear that she had worked out that there was something I was unwilling to share in there. At this moment, I remembered that the book was still in my bag, and I was therefore still carrying that monstrosity around with me. My bag suddenly became ten times heavier. "I sure would love to hear you read something sometime."

"Next week," I tell her honestly. "I'll have something new by then. The thing I was going to bring wasn't very good anyway."

"Hmm..." Lydia watched me carefully. It made me super uncomfortable. "I've already started on something killer after you gave me that prompt yesterday," she said, already dropping the suspicion.

She didn't specify what the prompt was, and I appreciated that. I didn't want to look like a total lunatic in a group of potential new friends.

"Is Charlie not eating lunch with you guys today?" I asked, attempting to change the subject.

Lisa put her book down, and all three girls leaned forward. "Charlie, eh?" Lisa asked with a wink. "You two seem to get along pretty well considering you're all new and stuff."

"That's a no then?" I asked, referring to my lunch question.

"Charlie usually goes home for his lunch," Lydia said. "Like a right loser. Sometimes he goes to the studio and helps Mum out. Too nice for his own good."

"You'll notice Tom is also nowhere to be seen," Lisa informed me. I actually hadn't noticed, which may have been a testament to how interesting Tom had been yesterday. "Tom is what we could refer to as a 'social butterfly,' flitting from friendship group to friendship group, collecting only the nectar that's to his taste and then moving on to the next—"

"Basically, he thinks he's too cool for us," Lydia translated. "But he needs stuff to put on his university applications, so he goes to a bunch of clubs, strives to be the best of the best, and is generally pleasant to everyone—"

"But won't acknowledge you anywhere outside of that club," Nadia finished.

I knew the kind well. My thoughts went back to my Glasgow friends. Back in my own school, I'd had plenty. Many of whom liked to act like my bestie in whatever class I was in or club I was part of or activity I was involved in. I could see now that my popularity back there was in part due to a best-selling mother and a father with friends in television. Now that one wasn't writing and the other wasn't around, none of my Glasgow friends seemed that bothered that I wasn't part of their lives anymore. Granted, one of them was now snogging my ex, so that was also probably a factor.

Here, however, nobody knew or gave a damn about who my family was. I was either That Girl in the Psycho House or The Writer Who Didn't Write Anything.

I couldn't work out whether that was better or worse than the people who pretended to like me.

Over the rest of lunch, the girls gave me a breakdown of the school. I was given the induction I had been denied by my brief period of notoriety during my first week. Lisa eventually left to go to band practice, and Nadia disappeared to vape with some other folk behind the bin sheds. Eventually, it was just Lydia and me, skulking towards our lockers.

Something pinged on my phone, and I grabbed it from my pocket. "New login on Spotify," it told me. My brow furrowed as I got hit with that wave of fear that follows thoughts like *oh my God, I've been hacked.* Clicking on "Devices," though, it looked like it had been a login from my PC at home.

Weird.

Maybe Mum was listening to something. My phone flashed and started playing "Heart-Shaped Box" by Nirvana. Loudly.

"Bugger," I mumbled, quickly cancelling it and shutting down Spotify.

"What was that?" Lydia asked, confused.

"I dunno, apparently my mum is stealing my Spotify and going through an angry grunge phase," I moaned and put my phone away. Silently, I decided it was time to change some passwords when I got home and did my best to put it out of my head.

On the way out of the cafeteria, Lydia hooked her arm in mine and walked me part of the way down the hallway. At the end, we could see Charlie hopping off his skateboard before a teacher could tell him off. The crowd swallowed him up quickly before I could wave.

Lydia leaned in towards my ear and whispered something important before she was swept off to class: "Be gentle on him; he's a sensitive soul."

To my surprise, Mum was waiting outside to pick me up after school. I was glad to see her and waved off Lydia, whom I was walking out with. A thank you was thrown Mum's way as I climbed in the car, and she was quick to ask if the girl I was with was a new friend. With more confidence than I've had in the last fortnight, I said yes.

At home, Mum led me straight into the kitchen. "Hey, you want to help me with some DIY pizzas?" she asked.

I took a sharp intake of breath. "DIY pizzas, Mum? Really?" I said. "Last time was a truly disastrous attempt."

"Well, I think we've both learned to keep it simple with the cheeses—mozzarella and cheddar. Avoid anything soft or blue at all costs."

"I thought we'd sworn off making our own pizza after the brie and meatballs incident?" I asked, skeptical of our last attempt.

"If I promise to be more conservative with toppings, will you help?"

"Sure, why not," I agreed.

We were both trying extra hard. It had been a difficult time lately, and maybe a distraction like destroying the kitchen with pizza was a good idea after all.

Mum continued, changing the subject. "Right, tell me about your writers' group. What did you take to read? Tell me everything."

"Oh, nothing. I forgot my notebook," I lied. My head was spinning a bit with what Lydia had said about her dad today, especially now that my mum was talking with her mum. I took a moment then decided to just ask. "Oh hey, did Charlie and Lydia's mum say anything about their dad? Lydia kind of dropped a bombshell today and told me he'd died a while back."

Mum also seemed to be undecided on whether or not to share something, but she eventually admitted that Charlie's mum had said something along those lines, but that she hadn't put two-and-two together until now.

"She didn't actually. They seem like a nice family," Mum said as she spread sliced mushrooms over my half of the pizza (she hated them herself, claiming that fungus is for forests, not for food). "I was wondering why Sara had chosen to stay near the kids' paternal grandparents and hadn't decided to go back to Spain. Maybe it makes them feel closer to him, having their grandparents nearby. Staying where her husband had grown up."

I nodded and added some extra cheddar over the top, assuming that only one type of cheese is simply unacceptable on a pizza—even after the last time. "You should start going to one of the dance classes," I said, half just an idea and half something I genuinely thought would be good. "Might help you make some friends here."

"You should start dating that boy," Mum said, throwing a tiny ball of dough at me. "Might get you out of this house."

"Shut it," I said, throwing a bit back. Like a competitive dodgeball player, she evaded the pizza ball with ease.

"Just goes to show you," Mum said. "Everybody's got their own drama going on. It's easy to just assume that you're the only one with something life-defining happening, but we're all just as stressed and worried all of the time."

"Yeah, alright, Dr Mum," I sighed with an overdramatic eyeroll.

"Well, I can't exactly give out dating advice anymore, can I?" She shrugged. There was flour in her hair and a smear of it across her cheek. "Might as well switch over to generic advice."

"Maybe you could start creating motivational posters?"

"Self-help books?"

"Fortune cookie fortunes?"

"At last, we're saved and can return to the life of luxury and excess we once held dear," Mum joked. "Right, let's get this beauty into the oven." Producing a pizza oven tray that I didn't even know we had, Mum put the monstrosity we had concocted in to cook, and we attempted to guess at how long

113

it should be in there for. Mum decided to go for her tried and tested method: leave it alone until it starts to look good.

"Oh," I said, suddenly remembering the Kurt Cobain cameo on my phone today, "I meant to ask. Did you use my Spotify today?"

"Nope," Mum said. "I've been listening to audiobooks all day. Why?"

"Nothing," I lied.

I tried to fight the panicked thought of *oh my God, I HAVE been hacked.* Definitely time for a password change.

We watched the *Great British Bake-Off* as we ate our not-altogether-too-awful DIY pizza and spent the entire episode saying, "I could do that; I just don't want to." Although, after a while, Mum started googling baking books and making ridiculous announcements.

"That's it," she declared, "I'm learning to make bread and we're eating fresh bread every day."

It is quite possible that Mum ordered a bunch of cookbooks that she had no intention of actually using. Just means she'd have to create a baking section in the library/dining room and keep them there. It'd add a little flavour to the shelves.

Pun intended.

You're welcome.

After dinner, I retreated upstairs to do some maths revision. Since we'd gotten here, I was really struggling with catching up with a maths class that was clearly much more advanced than the one I'd been in back home. I'd decided an hour or two of flicking through a textbook and quietly sobbing might help me somehow. It was only as I got to the doorway that I remembered that I hadn't actually set foot in here for, like, two days now. I'd spent last night in Mum's room.

When I opened the door, rage filled me as I saw something that only half-assured me that I wasn't crazy. The story that I'd written for the group was sitting neatly on my pillow. Dropping my bag at the door, I grabbed at the paper and inspected it thoroughly. It had been ripped from the book I'd initially written it in. The edges were torn, but it had been done carefully and with precision. I could never pull a page out of a notebook without tearing it in some way.

Even stranger, as I thumbed the corner of the page, I felt something. I ran my fingers over the paper. It felt as though something was there, like someone had been writing heavily on a page on top of this one, or had been writing with a ball-point pen that had run out of ink. There were clearly words inscribed onto the paper.

Retrieving my bag from where I'd abandoned it, I searched it for a pencil. Finding one (a Moomins pencil Mum had brought me back from a trip to London back when she'd had writing to actually talk to her agent about), I rubbed the pencil lightly over the engraving and watched the impression of letters appear under the grey of the lead:

THIS WAS TERRIBLE ANYWAY

I CAN MAKE YOU BETTER

. . .

It was only as I finished reading the words that I realised I'd been holding my breath the entire time. I didn't know how to feel about this. Scared? Angry? Confused? A mass of feelings tumbled around my head as I tried to make sense of what I was looking at. This was not my handwriting—one hundred percent.

A nonsensical idea came to me. I reached under the bed and grabbed at the Miles notepads, which were definitely multiplying as there were now four under here. To be honest, I'd kind of forgotten about them. I grabbed one I didn't recognise and opened it to a random page. Same handwriting.

I wasn't actually paying attention to the words as I compared my page and his. Just analysing the shape of the letters. But as my eyes readjusted and I started reading the text on this new pad, I was even more horrified.

I CAN HELP YOU, FLORA.

I CAN MAKE YOUR WRITING BETTER.

I DON'T EVEN MIND THAT YOU CALLED MY POETRY SHIT.

WELL, I DO ACTUALLY

AND YOU'RE WRONG.

I MEAN, I CAN HELP YOU WRITE SOMETHING BETTER

THAN THAT TRASH YOU CALLED A STORY.

. . .

I slammed the book shut and looked under the bed. There was something else back there as well as the other notepads. It was the yearbook. I grabbed the whole lot and threw them back into the cupboard. And then a weird hissing, whispering noise started. Right in my ear. Words that weren't words, just syllables and sounds. I gathered up all his shit and threw it into the cupboard. That's where he would stay for now.

I couldn't stay in my bedroom, so I went down to the library/dining room with my schoolwork. My heart was pounding the whole way, and my textbook shook with the tremble in my hands. Mum was perched on the comfy seat, under the good lamp, but I didn't care, I went over to the couch and threw myself down. I opened my textbook with a deep exhale and tried to let some of this gibberish settle in.

In all fairness, it would have been impossible for Mum to ignore this display, so I shouldn't have been surprised when she looked up from her book. "What's going on, sweetie?" she asked, eyeing me suspiciously.

"Nothing, just..." I thought carefully. How do I even put this into sensible words? A ghost boy is communicating with me through poor creative writing? That he'd been tearing up her books in an attempt to turn us against each other?

"That room's too weird to study in," I told her.

"Oh-kay..." Mum said and put her book down. "Do you want to elaborate at all?"

"Shhh." I hushed her and pointed at the maths book. "I'm trying to study."

Mum came to the decision that this was a good opportunity to do as I'd asked and shush, which was frankly just as weird as whatever was going on upstairs. She went back to her book, and I attempted to go back to mine. I glanced over at her and there was a little furrow in her brow as if there was something on her mind. We went on like this for some time.

At around eleven o'clock, I tried to pretend like I had fallen asleep in the hope that Mum would just put a blanket over me and let me sleep there like what sometimes happens in films. It always looked cute when it happened on screen. Unfortunately, though, Mum decided that beds are better places to sleep than couches, "woke" me up, and sent me to bed. I am not a good actress and had to poorly fake waking up. With any luck, she bought it.

I lingered in my bedroom doorway as Mum reached the bathroom before me.

"Mum," I said, catching her before she escaped to pee.

"Hmmm?" she said, flicking on the bathroom light. For the briefest moment, I imagined a shadow thrown against the fraction of the bathroom wall I could see. A tall, lithe figure had been waiting in the dark.

"Do you think this house is a bit...off?" I asked. I waited for her to berate me about my "Murder House" fears and yell at me about trying harder here.

But she didn't.

"I think it's taking me a little longer to settle in than I expected. So...maybe a little," she admitted.

Relief and fear grabbed at me from either side. The relief pulled me towards the thankful idea that my mum might believe me if I told her I thought there was a ghost boy rearranging things in my room. But fear pulled me towards the horrible idea that even Mum was a little frightened in here.

"Same," I agreed. "What do we do?"

"I don't know," Mum said with an uncomfortable smile. "Maybe just try a little harder to make it our home and not someone else's?" She shrugged. "What do I know though? Maybe we just need to sage the shit out of the place."

"Sage," I grumbled. "Right, you've lost me. Going to be now."

"Night, sweetie," Mum said and gave my arm a squeeze before heading into the bathroom, now devoid of strange shadows.

I'd been dreading returning to my bedroom. It'd reached a point where it wasn't really feeling like mine at all. There was a weight in the air and a substance to the shadows. I perpetually felt like there was someone waiting in the corners of the room—waiting for me to fall asleep so that they could whisper their worst thoughts to me.

That night, I attempted to sleep with the lamp on. It didn't work. The sleeping, that is—the lamp worked just fine. Although, it was prone to throwing shadows around the room, occasionally catching the shape of someone who was definitely not there.

Eventually, I tried to read a bit of my book club book until sleep eventually took me. As I started to close my eyes, the cupboard door creaked ever so slightly, reminding me that he was here.

Him

. . .

Emma Kathryn

They definitely both know I exist now. Although, it's fun to watch them avoiding telling each other. Mother and daughter do a little dance, each afraid of the other not believing or thinking they're mad. I thought they might blab last night but it never got that far. The worst that happened was that Flora relegated my belongings to the bedroom cupboard or sometimes, under the best. As if I care about her pushing me in either of these spaces. I've spent the last fifteen years in a cardboard box, a cupboard is an upgrade.

As usual, she's out of the house for school today. She really should log out of her computer, as well as use better passwords. It was easy to guess, considering all she talks about is this bloody book series. oph13—and she uses it for everything.

I've been enjoying this Spotify thing today. It does take all of my effort to type in band names, but it was worth it when I got it to work. I've listened to Nirvana, Linkin Park, and Seether. Actual music is something I've missed more than I realised. Lying on her bed, I spent all day imagining her with her headphones in, listening to it with me.

When I've got more strength, I'm going to make her a playlist. People don't make each other CDs or tapes anymore. It's all playlists. They're not half as romantic as burning a disc and writing the track list out yourself, but I guess it'll do.

While searching for updates on bands I like and skimming through some of their newest work, I learn something awful. Marcus, the lead singer from Etherwild – one of my favourite bands – died a few years ago. It looks like it was death by overdose. I read article after article after article about it. People passionately mourned him and wrote heartfelt things about his passing. Laney Fisher from the band FisherQueens had been his girlfriend—they were a band Stephanie had loved—and she'd written a whole album about losing him. It hurts to think that he's gone and that all these people suffered too.

Nobody talks about his death like my family did about mine, or even the way anyone used to talk about suicide fifteen years ago. Instead, they talk about mental health, support, and how to help someone in need, signs to look out for and numbers to call. In fact, every single article mentions mental health in some way, shape, or form.

Not one person ever asked about my mental health. There were no albums written about me. Instead, my mother had cried in this house and screamed that I was selfish for abandoning her. She'd packed what was left of me into a box and locked me away. I didn't get to live on in songs and other people's words. I've been forgotten and shunned.

It's not fair.

When Flora comes home, I beg for her to come upstairs. I need her right now. It feels like an eternity before she eventually appears. Tonight, I sit by her side and whisper. I've spent some of today crying and revisiting that pit I was in back when the house was empty. But when she's near, I feel a lightness. As if she can pull me back into the sun. I just need her to see that.

She knows that I helped with her story and, apparently, she's annoyed with me. It also seems to bother her that we're both living in this room. That will pass though when she sees what else I have in store for her. We'll live here together, forever. This is our space now and I'm more than happy to share it with her.

I wait until she falls asleep. It takes longer for her to sleep these days but tonight, she looked incredibly tired and didn't resist for long. Pushing the garbage book that she was reading aside, I make space. I lie in the bed, my one good hand pushing her hair out of her face and away from her ear. My mouth is so close to her face that it's almost unbearable. I wish she would open her eyes and see me.

Eventually, she turns on her side as if she's trying to block me out. Push me aside like a bad dream. But that won't help. It won't help at all.

I'm getting better at moving since I've left the box, and I reappear on the other side of the bed. She can't stop me that easily. Bothering her mother has been good practice, and I'm getting so much stronger.

I resume whispering and occasionally I let my lips brush her cheek while I'm telling her that she needs me and I need her.

She smells divine.

Chapter Eleven

Flora

Book club, as it turned out, was much more popular than the writers' group. Instead of the cosy group of five I'd been part of on Monday, there were now about a dozen readers in the library. The seniors were almost the same, minus Tom, who apparently felt that one literature-based club was enough for his UCAS forms. More third- and fourth-years filled seats, though. After reading the book (Mum and I are both gifted speed-readers), I could see why none of the first- or second-year kids were here. The book had some pretty mature themes. That was refreshing, though—my school library back in Glasgow had been a little short on good YA fiction.

I sat next to Lydia and Charlie, and they both greeted me with smiles. Lisa appeared to be reading another book by the same writer. Nadia was nowhere to be seen—apparently, this wasn't quite her thing. She didn't like being told what to read.

Charlie leaned in close and whispered, "I've read this book."

"Have you really?" I asked, genuinely surprised.

"No." He chortled. "Was that convincing though? I'm really hoping it was."

"I believed you. Although, in all fairness, you can see why I'd have thought you'd have read the book, considering you're sitting in a book club."

He lifted an iPad with a sticker saying *"Property of Blairness High Library"* on the back of it to reveal its screen open to a Twitter account, @blairnesslibrary. "Nah, I'm here to live-tweet the best comments. Mrs. Newman is convinced that if we go viral, then writers will want to come and do talks or something like that. I listen out for insightful comments and tweet them."

"You should start with 'I've read this book.' That's a good 'un."

He did an overdramatic fake laugh and then cut it short. "Live-tweeting book club is no joking matter, Ms. James. I take this role very seriously."

It was difficult not to let a real laugh escape me. I also became aware that Lydia was watching this entire exchange from the other side of the table. Charlie had also noticed this as well, and he and Lydia seemed to swap some kind of silent conversation, consisting of only eyebrow lifts and head tilts. Maybe it was a twin thing.

Mrs. Newman came in, and the session began. She wasn't the only adult there. A young teacher, Ms. Honey, also joined in. She barely looked twenty, and she was trying really hard. I knew that young teachers had to really fight for their jobs, and this meant signing up for loads of clubs and after-school sessions. It was like Tom with his university application, except Ms. Honey seemed to actually care about helping out. There was something kind of cool about her; she had cute shoes with cat faces on the toe, and her waistcoat was covered with enamel pins, which probably referenced odd hipster things I had never heard of.

Once the discussion started, I didn't have much to say—partly because I was currently being shackled by shyness, and partly because I was still living down the shame of standing up to read a story on Monday and then immediately sitting back down because a dead boy had switched it out for a poison pen letter. Besides that, a lot of the people here were very clever and had already stolen all of the things I was going to say.

Beside me, Charlie's thumbs moved rapidly. Every now and then, I would glance his way. At one point, his eyebrows leapt up and he lifted his head long enough to give Mrs. Newman a thumbs up as one of the fourth years said something equally clever about the expectations placed on young gay men by society. I nodded frantically. Lisa had a lot to say. *A lot.*

Forgetting that I was the newbie here and that Charlie was obviously skilled at being able to edit comments down to a single tweet, I leaned over to him after Lisa spoke and hissed: "You should tweet that bit. That was really cool."

He chuckled a little but didn't complain about my poor attempt at telling him what to do. He just nodded and said, "Sure thing," and got on with it. I felt like a bit of an idiot for jumping in, but I had just gotten so excited by the discussion.

We had nothing like this back in my old school. There had been some major budget cuts to the library, and our school librarian was only part-time. On the days when she wasn't there, the library was closed. Seeing how cool a school library could be suddenly made me feel really bad for everyone back home.

As the meeting was drawn to a close, it was decided that the next book would be *Midwinterblood* by Marcus Sedgwick, which sent me into a flurry of joy.

"I've read this book," I leaned over and told Charlie truthfully.

"So have I," he lied with a little wink as he shut the cover of the iPad over and it locked with a loud click.

Mrs. Newman and Ms. Honey had to do a little book negotiating with the rest of the group because the library only had four copies. Lydia shrugged and decided she'd just Kindle it. Lisa was keen to finish the book she was on and was happy to wait until someone had finished with one of the library copies. Everyone started to pack up as we prepared for the bell to ring for the end of lunch.

"Have you heard the good news?" Lydia asked me.

"Are the Spice Girls getting back together?" I joked. "For realsies?!"

"Unfortunately, not," Charlie said with a sad shake of his head. "But your Mum has signed up for a bunch of dance classes with my Mum. First of them starts tonight."

"Oh my," I said. This actually was news to me. I was kind of proud of her. "Is this when they'll start negotiating our betrothal?"

"I think in some cultures, this probably means you're married already," Lydia said with a disapproving hiss.

"Damn. My singleton lifestyle is over."

"You'd have to give it up sometime. Nobody can live like that forever."

"I sure gave it my best shot though."

The bell rang and Charlie, Lydia, and I thanked Mrs. Newman and started off towards class. Lydia vanished to get something from her locker. Students filled the halls around us and made our chat a lot less private.

"My mum has this weird thing where she's convinced if a young woman is home alone then she will spontaneously die, so she's asked if you want to come over and have dinner with Lydia and me," Charlie said.

The independent teen in me wanted to scream that I could handle myself and I'd been in alone plenty and lived to tell the tale but, truth be told, I hadn't been in the Murder House alone. The thought of being alone in that house made me feel a little sick. The thought of being alone with whatever was writing in my books and moving things genuinely made me feel like puking... when I say "whatever," I mean Miles. I just didn't like thinking about him.

"As unlikely as I am to spontaneously die, I may take you up on this generous offer. Purely out of curiosity since I want to see Lydia's goth bedroom," I agreed.

"Is that a yes then?"

"If only to keep our mothers happy."

"Of course."

Emma Kathryn

And just like that, I had kind of agreed to a date. A date that his twin sister would also be on.

Him

She hasn't come home yet.

Why isn't she home?

Chapter Twelve

Flora

Mum, on the other hand, had a very clear idea of what was going on. Almost exactly as the end of day bell went, Mum texted me:

Scored you a date tonight. You can thank me later. Away dancing.

What a charmer, my mother. I texted her back as I was standing at the school entrance, waiting for Charlie and Lydia.

I've told you before, you're my mother, not my pimp.

. . .

Lydia suddenly appeared by my side. The spectacular hat was making an appearance today, and her eyeliner was much more dramatic than I'd seen it at lunch.

"I hear you're visiting Casa de Burns this evening," she said. It seemed that she was telling me I was going rather than asking me.

"It would seem so," I replied, kind of excited by the prospect of the evening.

"Yeah, Charlie wouldn't shut up about it during last period," she told me. My heart fluttered a little. "Can't wait to show you the drama that is our decidedly not haunted house. It'll be a refreshing change for you."

I wasn't exactly planning on anything going down, so it didn't bother me too bad that this would be a chance to spend time with Lydia as well. I was really starting to like her. The group dynamic was starting to make more sense the more I spent time with them. Lisa and Nadia had their own priorities and tended to flit off whenever they needed to. Lydia didn't seem to have that in her. She was rooted in place like an old tree, and while everyone else seemed to perch on her branches for a bit, they would always fly off somewhere else eventually. Charlie was her constant, and she was fiercely protective of her twin brother.

As if on cue, he appeared before us. Charlie slid his skateboard under his arm. "I'd say hop-on, but it would seem that I brought the wrong kind of transportation for two people," he said.

"Walking is fine with me," I told him, and we started off through the village towards the cute little houses that were in the opposite direction of the monstrosity I had to live in.

On the brief, ten-minute walk to Lydia and Charlie's home (that's thirty minutes less than my usual forty, for those of you counting along at home), they both asked me about school in Glasgow and I was happy to tell them. I told them about my friends and the teachers and how much bigger my school had been compared to Blairness. When I told them about the kinds of trips we used to go on, Charlie was incredibly jealous. The Science Centre, Kelvingrove Museum, Glasgow Cathedral. According to Charlie, the best they ever got was a day on a farm, which apparently was a farm belonging to one of the girls in school, so it wasn't even much of a trip to her.

We arrived at a quaint little cottage with a wooden gate, which was set into a roughly hewn stone wall (granted, everywhere seemed to have roughly hewn stone walls here). The cottage in front of me looked like something out of a fairy tale. The garden was perfectly kept with little plant pots all the way up the path to the house. A few snowdrops and crocus poked their heads out of the soil in the clay pots, heralding that spring was just around the corner.

"Your house is really..." I began to say.

"Disgusting, right?" Lydia finished. "Imagine growing up somewhere that you'd find pictured on a shortbread tin."

"Hey, I live in the Psycho House," I reasoned. "I would rather live in a biscuit tin."

"Take that back now," she scoffed and elbowed my ribs.

There was something a little sickly sweet about it, I guess. It certainly wasn't the kind of home you could imagine a scruffy skater or would-be witch living in. Or maybe, this is exactly why they were both the way they were.

Charlie fumbled with his keys until Lydia eventually nudged him aside and opened the door with hers. She vanished into one of the rooms, yelling something about needing to get changed, leaving me standing in a small hallway. Charlie stepped past and urged me to follow him.

I looked around, seeing framed pictures everywhere of dancers, mid-waltz, mid-tango, and mid-celebration as they held up trophies and ribbons. There were cabinets in the hallway, filled to the brim with success. Trophies winked at me under the hall lights, and I squinted to read the tiny engravings.

"Oh my God," I gasped. "Your mum is a superstar."

Charlie shrugged. "She was. Now she's a teacher in a tiny town. Hey, maybe once she's through with your mum, *she'll* be the next superstar."

"My mum, a dancer?" I shook my head as I stepped away from the cabinet. "Nah. Just a very lonely ex-romance writer."

"There is plenty of romance in the dance," Charlie said with a wink.

"Bloody hell, that's the cringiest thing you've ever said," Lydia said from the stairs. She'd changed quicker than my record-breaking time and was now wearing dark jeans and a long floaty top with vampire sleeves. Her make-up had been hastily touched up as well. It was almost as if she was trying to impress me.

I smiled. "You look fancy out of school uniform!"

"How dare you," Lydia said, dripping with sarcasm. "I've got a girlfriend in Inverness. I'm spoken for. Anyway, you're supposed to be hitting on Charlie."

I saw the embarrassment bubble up in Charlie's face before Lydia grabbed my hand and pulled me up the stairs. "Now come with me if you want to live."

"Sure," I agreed, and followed dutifully.

"Charlie, get dinner on," Lydia barked, and I could feel the rage coming from her brother at the bottom of the stairs. But he said nothing and disappeared from my sight as we went upwards.

More photographs of a young couple, whom I now understood to be Lydia and Charlie's parents, lined the staircase. They looked absolutely stunning. Bright costumes and sparkling make-up festooned every image. The lives they lived before parenthood were exciting ones. The lack of pictures of their children showed how much Sara yearned for that life and how much she missed her husband.

Lydia decided that it was time for the tour. The first stop was Charlie's room. There were road signs on his room door. Inside, the walls were covered in posters for films and video games. *Ex Machina, Dredd, Mad Max, The Witcher, Life is Strange, Overwatch.* I smiled and fought the urge to run my hand over the *Overwatch* one. Crossing the room to the desk, I gave his PC setup a nosy. It was much fancier than mine. His headphones were perched atop the monitor, and he had one of those ridiculously edgy light-up keyboards—the kind that are obnoxiously noisy and that I would probably throw out the window after a loss on competitive mode on *Overwatch.* I took a mental note to mock him for this later.

By his bedside table, a bunch of polaroid pictures were pinned to a corkboard (which probably should have been nailed to the wall, but was instead on the floor and propped against it). I studied them closely. There were at least three of either him and Lydia or just Lydia herself. Another was of him and a bunch of skateboarding lads, showing off some "Sick Moves."

It reached a point though when I didn't know how much snooping was acceptable. I mean, I'd only known Charlie for two weeks and here I was, standing in his bedroom, checking out the life he has had up until the moment we met outside school and awkwardly nodded.

"So, that was the loser's room," Lydia groaned as she shepherded me back into the hall.

In my pocket, my phone buzzed. It was Mum saying that she'd just arrived at class and hoped I was doing okay. I knew that this didn't really need a response. It was more her making a point that she'd actually gone out and done something today. Part of me was kind of pleased for her, while the other part was a little embarrassed that she had chosen my new friends' mum's dance class as a way to get over Dad.

Lydia pulled me into her bedroom with the excitement of a thirteen-year-old hosting her first sleepover. I found myself standing in the middle of Lydia's bedroom, staring at the tapestry-draped walls and gothic art prints dotted around the room. The inside of the door was plastered with home-made protest signs about women's rights, LGBTQ+ rights, climate change, and saving the bees. Her bedsheets were beautiful mandalas in dark purples, navy blues, and silvers. Crystals of different colours and sizes adorned her windowsill. A palm-reading hand-statue thing sat on her dressing table but seemed to be used more to hang jewellery than for reference.

She fidgeted as I looked around. Flicking through tarot cards, she tried to look busy as I took it all in. It was incredibly cool in here.

"Wow," I gushed. "You're really into the whole witchcraft thing, right?"

"It's my Spanish *bruja* blood." She smirked. "Even if Mum is like *that's not a thing*! It's totally a thing."

"My room looks like nobody lives there right now," I admitted, a little sad.

Lydia sat down on the chair in front of her desk. It was covered in books, plastic skulls, and eye shadow palettes. There was literally no room to work on that desk; I have no idea where she got any of her writing done. Sitting right at her elbow, not surprisingly, were three incredibly battered and well-loved books—the *Archival Cycle*.

"You've only just moved in." She gestured around the room. "This kind of mess takes years of dedication."

"I guess I just miss the Glasgow house."

"But now you have a beautiful new spooky house to make your own."

"There is absolutely nothing beautiful about that house," I told her in all seriousness. "It kind of sucks."

"Anywhere new sucks," she said. "I'd love to help you make it yours. Like your room, that is. We could have a painting party. Make it look wicked again. Paint out all the bad vibes."

"That actually does sound cool. Thanks. I mean, my mum might be like *God no,* but I'll ask."

"I'll get my mum to plant the idea while they're dancing—make her think it'll be good for your sad, lonely soul."

"Am I a sad, lonely soul?" I asked and sat on the floor beside the bed, opposite Lydia.

"You do give off that aura."

"Wow, thanks."

At this point, Charlie appeared. Like his sister, he'd gone for a speedy make-over too. His white uniform shirt had been switched for a *Dungeons and Dragons* t-shirt (*"This item grants the bearer +2 to Charisma"*), and his school trousers had been swapped for skinny jeans. They could not have been comfortable to skateboard in. He slumped down to sit next to me and blew his hair out of his eyes.

"Hey," he said to me, coolly trying to regain his composure.

"Oh, hi there," I smiled.

"Welcome to the madhouse," he said with a shake of his head. Lydia waved her arms as if joining in on his welcome party.

"Everybody's batshit in here," she added.

"This isn't mad," I informed them. "My mum cries when Netflix emails her to tell her about a new show she'd like."

"That's pretty weird," Charlie said.

"It really is."

"Like, for no reason, or what?"

"My dad ran off and left us for a Netflix show," I told them. "The *Archival* show."

This might have been the first time that I actually admitted this both to someone else and to myself. Lydia sat up a bit, as if she realised that the joking was done. I could see she wanted to ask about the show, but she knew now wasn't the time.

I continued, "Turns out my dad is a bit of a dick. He's dating someone who works on the show. I kind of blamed Mum for a bit, but now *I* feel a bit of a dick for giving Mum a tough time. When I should really have been giving *him* the tough time."

"I'm sorry," Lydia said.

"It's okay. Not your fault."

"Nah, but it still sucks."

"Thanks."

We sat quietly leaning against Lydia's bed. Me: acknowledging that my dad was an asshole. Them: probably trying to work out how to process this information.

"So, who told you about our dad's accident?" Charlie asked, not looking even remotely annoyed. "Lydia?" The twins exchanged another one of their silent conversations.

I opened my mouth and a lie sat perched on the end of my tongue, ready to be spoken, but he deserved better than that. I swallowed it over and told him the truth. "Yeah."

"Yeah, she would." He sighed heavily beside me and seemed to be going over what to say in his head.

"It's not a big dark secret, Charlie," Lydia said. "We only have one parent because our dad is dead. Flora only has one parent because her dad ran away to shag someone at Netflix." She turned to me. "You can't walk around this house without feeling him everywhere. He's our ghost."

"You know, you don't have to tell me anything you don't want to," I reasoned. "Just because I like to overshare doesn't mean you have to."

"No," he said, turning to me and smiling a little. "It's fine. It's just..." Another sigh. Lydia nodded at him like it was okay to talk. "Okay, so my parents were both superstar dancers. Ballroom dancing, not like popstar backing dancers or anything like that."

"Wouldn't that have been cool?" Lydia mused.

"Professionals through and through. And then they met each other and started to dance together. Somehow, they both got even better and then they were winning everything. Like basically, they were the Venus and Serena of dancing—but not related, because that would be super weird. Then they had us, and they just kept on winning stuff."

"Well, Dad kept on winning stuff," Lydia interrupted. "Mum decided to take a break and look after us. Twins are a freaking nightmare, I'm sure. They moved here to be near Dad's parents. I'm guessing they needed our grandparents for babysitting and stuff. But Dad missed the thrill of it and went back. Without Mum."

"I mean, they needed the money though, Lydia," Charlie jumped in. "They couldn't both not work."

"Yeah, but then Dad got a new dancing partner and was conveniently away more and more and more."

"One day, Dad was driving to a competition. Some idiot drunk driver ploughed into the car. Dad was instantly killed. And that's that."

Lydia leaned on the back of her chair as if just telling this story was exhausting. It seemed like they were both missing bits out.

"What about your mum's career?" I asked.

Charlie ran his hand through his hair and shook his head a little. "Mum decided that she couldn't dance without Dad, even though dancing is her life. Instead, she set up the studio. She acts like she's happy enough with that, but I don't know."

"I'm sorry," I said. Mum's words about not realising how much people had going on in the background hit home.

I suddenly became very aware that I was in Lydia's bedroom on her bed, and we were all being soul-bearingly honest. We were so close that our shoulders were practically touching. I tried to remember if we'd started that close, or if we'd been working our way closer and closer. There was a brief moment where I thought that Charlie was wondering about it too. For an even briefer second, I could actually feel him drawing closer.

That is, until Lydia jumped to her feet and pulled me up with her. "Enough of this misery business. Let's eat. Charlie, I'm assuming you're burning something as we speak?"

Any spark that was starting to ignite between us was quickly doused. We both giggled and got up. Lydia grinned at me, hiding her sadness. A little flicker of Charlie hid in her eyes.

It made me a little jealous that I'd never had a sibling, but I had grown up pretty spoiled and very close to Mum. We probably wouldn't have been that close if there had been another me to vie for her attention.

We entered the kitchen, and it was way more interesting than ours. Granted, there wasn't an equal ratio of unopened packing boxes to empty wine bottles. Family photos seemed to find their place in here rather than on the walls of the hallways. The pictures were all over the fridge. In fact, the side of the fridge was practically a whole family tree encased in ceramic magnets. Almost every single one featured someone either laughing at the funniest thing they'd ever heard or chomping down on something delicious. Food and fun: that's what this family seemed to be all about. I sat down at the table in the centre of the room and took in the warmth.

Charlie followed us in and plugged his phone into some speakers. Early 2000s pop-punk started blasting. It was exactly what I expected from the skater, and a grin found its way onto my face.

"Spaghetti carbonara it is," Charlie announced, pulling a simmering pot off the hob. He stopped and turned, looking at me expectantly. "What are you doing still on your butt?" he asked indignantly.

"What?!" I laughed. "I'm a guest!"

"Oh no." He shook his head. "You're sous chef tonight." He pointed at the stove with a piece of dry spaghetti, which was doubling up as a pointer.

"Yes sir," I agreed and got to my feet.

I had never actually made spaghetti carbonara, so I considered this a good way to widen both my culinary repertoire and Mum's. To the tunes of "Check Yes Juliet" and "I Write Sins Not Tragedies," Charlie and I put together a meal that was acceptable to Lydia's standards and talked nonsense the whole time. Lydia scrolled through her phone from the table and occasionally recited witty banter she found on Twitter.

When the food was ready, Lydia grabbed plates and the three of us moved around the kitchen as if we'd known each other forever. In no time, we were all seated around the table, eating, drinking, and bitching about school. Lydia gave me the rundown of which teachers to avoid and how to keep some others sweet. They chatted about local stuff, too: which cafes were nice, and when to get the bus into Inverness for a decent day out.

Wiping up the last of my sauce with a slice of garlic bread, I polished off my meal. It has been pretty damn tasty. Apparently, I was a good sous chef. Charlie was an even better head chef.

Then, Lydia threw me a curveball. "Do you dance?"

"Oh no," I replied.

"Charlie is a good dancer. The best of the both of us."

Now I did laugh. "I thought you were kidding when you said that you have to demonstrate in your Mum's classes!"

"I never kid," he said with a smile. "We're ballroom born and bred in this house. Literally."

"But you skateboard, and wear baggy shirts, and listen to Fall Out Boy!"

"And I could waltz you all round this house." Now, there was a slight air of cocky assuredness to his voice. Bravado had entered to the Burns' kitchen. This was a side I'd never seen in Charlie, and I think I kind of liked it. I could see his sister in him when he was like this.

Lydia grinned and saw an opportunity. "Charlie, come on then. Teach the girl something," she announced and pointed at me.

Charlie shook his head. He ran a napkin over his mouth and pushed his bowl away. "Not a chance, *bruja*."

"Yes!" she cheered.

"No, no, no," I repeated.

"Yes, yes, yes!" she mimicked.

Scrambling off the chair, Lydia bounded across the room and snatched at Charlie's phone. The music—she was trying to reach the music. At this point, Charlie snapped into action. They tousled for the choice of tunes, and Lydia won supreme.

"This music isn't dancing music," she muttered, as she scrolled through Spotify.

My insides were already starting to jig. I couldn't dance and now my new best friend was going to force me to learn how to from her brother, a boy I may have been developing a crush on.

"Dumb music," Lydia grumbled. Then her eyes lit up. She smirked at Charlie and whispered the word, "Salsa."

With the tap, Green Day stopped singing about American Idiots and a Latin beat took over. I thought I recognised the voice, but I wasn't sure.

"Is that Enrique Iglesias?" I asked with a laugh.

Charlie sighed. "Enrique is to Mum what Paulo Nutini was to Dad," he explained in a way that didn't actually explain anything.

"Teach!" Lydia instructed.

"Looks like we're dancing," Charlie said and offered me a hand. Tentatively, I took it, and he pulled me to my feet.

"Fast, fast, fast, slow," Lydia ordered.

"Ssssh," Charlie hissed at her. "You have to show. You can't just yell stuff."

"Then show!" Lydia stood at our sides and helped us get into stance. It reminded me of the scene in *Dirty Dancing* where Penny was helping Baby get ready for taking her place.

Nerves overtook me, and I let go of his hand. He didn't try to grab it back. "I don't know if this is a good idea," I complained. Around the room, Enrique Iglesias began to croon.

"Nah, it's easy," Charlie said, not really getting what I was trying to say.

Then he slipped out of skater mode and into this supple dancing boy. One leg seemed to elongate, and his baggy t-shirt skimmed his hips as he found his stance.

"Okay, so I need you to mirror me. We're going to go quick or we're going to have to start the song from the beginning," he said.

"Wait, what?"

"Eyes on me," he ordered and pointed at his face. I hadn't noticed how deeply brown his eyes were until now. As he spoke, he slowly demonstrated. "We'll start side-to-side. So, we're going to step out to your right, rock back on the left then step back to the middle. Hold for a beat. Then do the same on the other side." I was watching his feet closely. That is, until his hand found my chin and lifted it up to look at his face again. "You have to feel the music," he informed me. "Count the beat. That'll keep you on track. Watching your feet will just get you flustered."

Lost for words, I nodded and started to count. He led me through the steps again and it suddenly didn't seem so scary. He then talked me through the back-and-forth steps. After only a little bit of trying, he was smiling and nodding. "You're getting it. Now you've got to put a little flair in…"

The music stopped, and we both looked to Lydia. "Start from the beginning," she said and suddenly, I could see both her mother and her father in her. The faces in the pictures were practically in the room with us, and I felt like I had stepped into their childhood.

The music started again, and we stood beside one another. By now, the table had been pushed away and we had plenty of space. It became clear that this was the kind of house where the furniture was regularly ditched in favour of a dance floor.

The lines were cheesy as the song started, but Charlie played along and mouthed along enthusiastically. We started off standing apart, repeating the side-to-side steps. After only one verse, I found myself getting into it. I shook my hips and rolled my shoulders. Never had I ever done anything like this. It was an absolute riot.

As the second verse began, Charlie took my hands and pulled me close. We were in a stance we had tried and as he sang along, he took the lead, and we moved through the front to back steps. We were way closer than we ever had been; I could breathe him in at this distance. He stared me down as he passionately mouthed the words to the song—something about love being just a phase. Our hands meshed, and I imagined that he gave me a little squeeze.

It was at that point that I finally accepted that I was crushing hard.

"Mi amor!" a voice screeched from the kitchen door. Charlie and I leapt apart as though we had been electrocuted. Lydia laughed like it was the funniest thing she had ever seen. We spun around to see both of our mothers standing in the doorway. "Look at you two!" Charlie's mum, Sara, sang. A grin was plastered across my own mum's face, which was red and sweaty from all the dancing she had been doing.

"Mum!" Charlie moaned.

We stole a quick glance at each other and then turned away a little too dramatically. Lydia gathered up the dinner plates, smiling at me like she had just learned my terrible secret. I stormed across the room to grab Mum by the arm and pull her out into the hallway.

"Thanks for dinner," I yelled behind me, abandoning any goodbyes from Lydia or Charlie.

"See you again next week, Sara." Mum laughed as we left the kitchen, being followed by Sara. Unfortunately, I couldn't make the speedy exit I wanted and had to stop at the staircase where my bag and jacket hung from the banister.

Both women beamed intently at me as I pulled my jacket on. I felt like I was melting under their gaze.

"Please don't say anything," I grumbled and made my way towards the door. I spotted the mums trying to secretly make an *"I'll call you"* gesture at one another before saying goodbye and waving one another off.

Mum practically glowed the whole way to the car, and then kept glowing the entire time it took me to get into my seat and do my seatbelt up. She refused to start the car until I looked at her.

"Am I good at fixing you up, or am I good at fixing you up?" she asked, filled with smug pride.

"That's enough from you, Mother," I groaned and tried to sink as far down into my seat as I could.

Once I was sure that she had stopped looking at the car pulled away, I let a secret smile creep onto my face, where it settled for the rest of the journey home.

Him

Where.

Is.

She?

Chapter Thirteen

Flora

Once we were back in the house, Mum wouldn't shut up. She was obviously desperate to ask me about my intimate dance lesson and dinner with my newfound besties, but knew that I wasn't going to spill yet. Instead, she spoke at length about her own class, about how nice the people were, and about how much she sees herself becoming good friends with Sara.

As embarrassed as I still was, I was pleased to see my mum like this—happy. She was in gym clothes—leggings and a loose-fitting sleeveless top—and she was chugging water like it was wine. As she buzzed around our kitchen, she babbled about the things she did and the people she met. I, on the other hand, sat at the kitchen table and toyed with my phone.

I flicked open Twitter. Closed it again. Flicked open TikTok. Closed it again. Buzzfeed. Closed. My thumb hovered over IMDB. I did not click it.

Eventually, Mum sat down in front of me. She stopped talking long enough to let us both breathe. We made eye contact and smiled.

I nodded.

That was enough.

Mum decided that a shower was in order. I agreed and she threw her empty water bottle at me. I stayed in the kitchen and stared at my phone. I willed myself not to open my messages and start typing a message to Charlie. Instead, I opted to text Lydia, whose number I had nabbed during book club. I sent a brief one:

Hey, thanks for tonight. Your room is aaaaamazing.

She instantly responded with:

Paint party, let's do it

Followed by a GIF of the "painting the roses red" scene in *Alice in Wonderland*. I smiled and fought not to text Charlie.

In a weak attempt to distract myself, I opened YouTube and fired up a "Salsa for Beginners" video. It looked terrible on my phone, and I felt stupid, so I decided to go upstairs and try on my computer. Then I could pretend that I wasn't going to practice with my bedroom door shut.

The video was still playing as I walked up the stairs. The shower was running, and I could hear Mum attempting to sing in the bathroom—it sounded like somebody really was being tortured in this house. While watching a pair of professionals demonstrate some swishy fancy moves that Charlie had apparently deemed too advanced for my virgin feet, I pushed my bedroom door open.

My nose was instantly assaulted by a smell so bad that I dropped my phone in a desperate attempt to cover my face. It was a strong musty smell, tinged with something rotten. I turned my gaze upwards.

"Holy crap," I gasped from between my fingers.

On the ceiling was a large, darkening stain. From it, some clear liquid dripped down onto my bed. Directly onto my pillow.

I must have started screaming for Mum at this point, and she came running into the room in a towel and dripping shower gel. Her dressing gown was half-on, and she was frantically pulling at the rest of it. She was yelling something at me, but I couldn't hear her. Instead, I pointed at the bed.

"Holy crap," she echoed as everything came flooding back to me. Now she was covering her nose. "The shower didn't do this, right?" she asked, looking up at the stain.

Shaking my head, I remembered how to speak again. "No. And I don't think it was there this morning."

Being the kind of woman who wasn't afraid of anything, Mum stepped into the room and grabbed the pillow. The slow drip continued, but this time hitting my bed. Doing the most stupid thing I could ever imagine, Mum decided to sniff the pillow. It didn't get very close to her face before she yanked it back.

"Christ," she hissed. "Why does your room smell like a teenage boy who's never washed?"

"Or a dead one?" I suggested.

"Please don't say the words 'Murder House'," she complained. As if it would destroy the offending smell (which was still creeping in via the ceiling), she quickly started yanking the pillowcase off. What lay beneath was worse.

We both gasped as beneath the cover, a bloody red bloom blossomed on the pillow.

"Oh my God, Flora," Mum cried. "Is this yours? What happened?"

"This isn't my blood," I whispered. The blood sure didn't look fresh. It looked like a stain that had happened years ago and dried and had been forgotten about. Or pushed away, hidden under a pillowcase, and ignored. Had I been lying on this? How long had this been under the cover?

Even though my Mum had made a career out of fluffy romance, she was incredibly clever. She had razor-sharp analytical skills, which was why she wrote historical novels. She liked the research and the level of work put in to keep things accurate. Then, she painted over it with delicious marshmallow fluff and wrote happy endings instead. But here, she had her investigating face on. Reaching for the bed, she yanked the top of the sheet down. Sure enough, beneath where the liquid was now falling onto the sheet, a dark crimson mark was starting to form.

"Mum..." I tried to whisper but only squeaks came out.

"Right, give me a second," she said, before vanishing from my room.

I stood alone, staring at the bloody pillow and trying to pretend like I didn't know where this was coming from. Tears fell and it felt like someone was gripping my chest tightly, whispering in my ear that I didn't have to breathe so much, not really. I tried to take a deep breath and instead, the air shuddered in my chest, struggling to go where it was supposed to.

Behind me, I was sure I could hear that hissing noise that only partly sounded like real words. This time, I was sure that it was saying my name.

Flora...

Flora...

This is for you...

...a gift...

Lie down...

...Lie down with me...

Something was forcing my eyes closed. I tried to blink it away and shook my head. My eyelids fluttered. A sharp white light burst in front of me when I tried to open them. Searing pain shot through my head, stabbing at my eyes and ears.

Lie down...

"Flora, sweetie," Mum said, grabbing me by the shoulders and suddenly taking all the noise and pain away. Opening my eyes, the light was gone. The noise was gone. Everything was back to normal. I looked at Mum, and she had pulled on jeans and a T-shirt. "You're not looking good," she told me, inspecting me in that way mums do when you're sick and they're mentally running through the four hundred million things that could be wrong with you (always convinced of the worst ones first).

"I'm okay," I lied. She knew that I was lying, but she was in problem-solving mode. I imagined her marking down *"cure sick daughter"* onto her internal to-do list.

"Attic," she announced and pulled down the ladder faster than I could tell her to stop.

"Mum," I said, still feeling a little woozy. "Please don't."

"We've got to find this leak," she commanded and disappeared up the ladder. Reluctantly, I followed. I was only halfway up the ladder when I heard her yell, "What the fu..."

As I stepped into the attic space, I saw what horrified her so. Right in the spot where I had originally found it, the Miles box sat. Directly above where my bed would be, of course.

"I binned that and everything that was in it," Mum said. I wasn't sure if she was telling me this (which I already knew, having watched her do so at the weekend) or if she was trying to convince herself that it had really happened.

"I know," I agreed. Again, not sure if I was now saying it to reassure her or if I was trying to reassure myself that I'd seen all of these items go into the bin.

Cautiously, she approached the box. I followed. For a little while, we both stared down at it. The smell was definitely coming from this. It was even worse up here.

I don't really know what made me take the lead on this one, but I crouched down and opened the box. Everything was back in there. The jacket, the CDs, the yearbook, and all the multiplying notepads. I reached down to pick one up. One of the newer ones that had been filled with messages for me. A sharp pain shot up my left arm and I recoiled.

"Flora!" Mum yelled and grabbed my wrist. A large red wound was embedded into my forearm. Blood began to seep out and pool on my skin. A drop fell into the box.

We both looked down to discover the broken aftershave bottle, now tainted with my blood, as well as the offending scent. My arm stung like hell. Mum wrapped her hand tightly around it, not having any kind of bandage handy and not trusting anything else in the box. This hurt even more, and I tried to wriggle away like a tiny child being forced to take medicine she didn't like.

"We need to take you downstairs," Mum said, applying even more pressure. I hissed and tried not to swear. "But I swear all of this was in the bins. I broke that bottle when I dropped it."

I watched her trying to solve this. Her eyes kept darting between the box and the ladder down to the hall.

"It wasn't all in the bins," I admitted. "I had the yearbook and one of the notepads. But then there were more notepads when I came home from school one day. They were in my cupboard. They weren't in the bin."

Somehow, Mum looked even more horrified. I considered telling her about what was in the notepads and the fact that something I had written had been switched out for something

I didn't even remember writing. Maybe we could wind up on the same page that way.

An idea seemed to come to Mum, and I felt a wave of relief, as if some kind of burden was about to be lifted. "The estate agent's boy," she said, looking like she had just cracked the mystery and had pulled the scary mask off of the old caretaker.

I'd have gotten away with it too. If it wasn't for you meddlin' romance writer and your dumb kid.

"You said there was a boy at school who was trying to tell you the place was haunted," she continued in her Sherlock Holmes-style concluding monologue. "He was the estate agent's son. Who else might have a key for this place that we don't know about? An estate agent..."

"Mum..." I tried to interrupt but she wasn't having any of it.

"He swipes a key, lets himself in and moves things around to try to continue that Psycho House rumour he's been spreading—"

"How do you know about the Psycho House thing?" I successfully interrupted her this time.

"Oh sweetie, you know I follow you on Twitter. And I looked into it on that day you were slamming and banging your way around the house."

"If I weren't bleeding profusely right now, I'd give you a rant about online privacy."

This seemed to remind her I was injured, and we descended the ladder. We retreated to the bathroom, and I was thoroughly bandaged up. Mum was still on ridiculous theories (granted, mine was even more ridiculous).

"That's it. It's that pig of a boy letting himself in and trying to mess with you," she said as she fixed the bandage in place. I was sitting on the closed toilet seat and Mum was perched on the edge of the bath. "I'm talking to his mother tomorrow."

"No, Mum," I insisted. "Please, for the love of all that is holy, please don't do this. That boy's all froth and no milkshake. There's no way he did this."

"Flora, sweetie, someone has been in this house. Even if it's not him, she's the only one who has had a key lately. Or she might even be able to find out if it's the previous owners. Maybe someone is letting themselves in and forgetting that they don't live here anymore."

"Do you hear yourself?"

"Well, what are you suggesting?!" Mum snapped.

"I don't know," I lied. I knew that I couldn't say the word 'ghost' out loud. "I just don't know."

Once Mum and I had sufficiently bandaged me up, we took the box back outside. I didn't sneak out any notepads this time, and I certainly didn't want to look at the yearbook again. It was incredibly dark outside. Standing in the murky garden really hammered home how far away we were from everyone else in town. Mum shovelled the contents of the box into the bin for the second time. She didn't bother with recyclables this time, though—they were all thrown in with the general waste.

Emma Kathryn

I stood in the dim light that leaked out from the kitchen door and windows and surveyed the vast blackness before me, cradling my sore arm as I did. This was the first time I had taken a proper look around the back of the house. It was difficult to make much out, but I could tell that it was wildly overgrown and that there was a large old tree in the furthest corner of the fenced-in yard. There was also something under the tree that I couldn't quite identify.

Crossing the thick vegetation, I made my way over to the unknown shape. After only a few steps, I was out of the comforting glow of the kitchen and into the shadows.

I heard Mum call my name, but I was set on working out what was hiding there. The closer I got, the more I could see that it was a long object, with tree roots curling around the bottom edges and a layer of leaves covering the surface. As I stepped within a couple of feet of it, I could finally work out what it was.

It was an old bath.

On one side, it was covered in what I imagined was rust or a dark stain—I couldn't be sure in the darkness. At the base, some kind of family of insects moved around. A spider's web hung from between the hot and cold taps. The web was adorned with two unlucky insects. Only one was still moving, though—a ladybird, I imagined (there was no way I could be sure in this light). The other had given up entirely. It might have been dead already.

The wind picked up and tossed my hair around. As it brushed my ears, the hissing voice came back.

Lie down here with me...

Mum's hand landed on my shoulder, and I jumped with fright.

"Come on, sweetie," she said. "Sleepover tonight until I get rid of that funky mattress and pillow on your bed."

I had almost forgotten that my bed would be inhabitable tonight. Silently, I cursed our unseen tormentor. I loved that mattress—it had been incredibly comfortable.

"We can top and tail it," Mum continued, leading me back inside.

I stole one last look at the bath graveyard at the bottom of our garden. I'm not sure if it was tiredness, stress or blood loss, but I saw the tree branches and the rest of the wild vegetation morph into the shape of a person, sitting in that dead bathtub.

Mum slammed the kitchen door shut behind us. I was almost sure that maybe she had seen it too.

Him

I've done something stupid. Flora, my darling. I didn't mean to hurt you. I was just so angry.

Angry that you didn't come home when I was expecting you to. Angry that you've replaced me with stupid, dumb friends who will never love you like I do. Angry that you still won't see me.

That friend is bad news. The girl. I know what the boy is after, but the girl makes my skin crawl. Flora doesn't need friends like that—ones that keep her out all night and away from me. All the constant texting and laughing. I'm sick of it. I'm sick of her laughing at other people's jokes and listening to their stories and the other bullshit they talk about. She should be talking to me. She should be listening to me. I'm the one who really understands her.

I watch as her mother tries to wrap her arm. A slight pang of guilt strikes me, but if she hadn't have stayed out all evening with those so-called friends, ignoring me, then I wouldn't have gotten angry. It was stupid of me, but it was her fault too.

I watch as they try to dispose of me again. It won't work. Especially not now.

You've bled on me now, Flora. We are one. I can feel your heartbeat where mine used to be. You're mine. You always will be.

In the darkness of the garden, I lie in wait. For a second, I was so sure that she saw me. She holds her arm where I have branded her. A mark that shows the world she's mine.

Across the garden, we have a moment. I think she can finally see.

Chapter Fourteen

Flora

Call me cynical, but I couldn't help but feel that some of the effort Mum put into fixing my ruined bed and investigating the *Psycho House Ghost Mystery* could have been put into writing—you know, doing her actual job that we need to pay the bills. Somehow, in the space of just two days, Mum managed to replace my mattress, pillows, and bedsheets, which seemed to be no mean feat, considering we lived in the arse end of nowhere. I was lost as to how she managed to do this so fast.

On Friday (or "Mattress Day" as Mum had christened it), things were starting to go back to normal. That night, I would get to sleep in my own bed and nothing weird had happened in the house since then. Thursday had been pretty straight-forward at school, and I'd even seen Lydia and Charlie a couple of times. Charlie had taken to sending me songs since Wednesday night. They were all headed with a message stating: "Better than Enrique Iglesias". Of course, this meant that I had taken to responding with other songs that were all headed "Better than..." followed by literally every band he sent me. It was all kinds of adorable.

Lydia had created a Pinterest board of bedrooms she thought I might like. She had also started sending me outrageous *Archival Cycle* theories I had never read before, and we started to come up with our own.

Today though, I sat at lunch with the girls and my two quiet days were quickly turned upside down. It was nearly the end of lunch, and Lydia and Nadia were debating what to put in this week's zine while Lisa was reading the next book club book on her Kindle.

Keeping my phone under the table, I sent Charlie the song "Final Song" by Mo, informing him that this was the last one he was getting today. Lydia glanced at me every now and then and I was pretty sure that she knew who I was messaging. My phone buzzed and the message said *Better than Enrique Iglesias – "In the End" by Black Veil Brides* and was accompanied by a YouTube video of a heavily made-up boyband with an attitude problem. I giggled, and Lydia definitely clocked me this time.

Before she had the chance to sass me, a voice rang out across the cafeteria, quickly getting closer and closer to us.

"Hey, Psycho House!" Damn. Phil the Dude stormed up to our table and kicked my chair so that I was facing him. Lydia sprang to her feet, although I'm not quite sure what she was planning on doing. "You want to explain why your crazy mother is telling my mum that I've been breaking into your house and moving stuff around?"

In that moment, I desperately wished for the world to kill me. Maybe the ceiling would crash down on me, or Phil would just destroy me like he undoubtedly wanted to.

"What is this?" he continued. "A really shit attempt at getting back at me because everyone thinks you're an utter weirdo?"

The canteen went quiet. Well, about as quiet as a school canteen can go when there are teenagers in it. I scrambled for words, but they weren't happening.

"Hey, buddy," a voice said behind Phil.

He stepped aside to reveal Charlie. He must have just arrived back at school and was coming in to meet us. Dread filled me as I imagined Charlie taking a kicking from Phil the Dude in a pointless attempt to defend my honour.

"Why don't you just leave her alone and go back to your friends?" Charlie tried to reason sensibly.

Phil took a step closer to Charlie. Compared to Charlie, who was lithe and average height for a guy, I could see now see how tall and built Phil was. He really was about to endure a kicking for me. I couldn't let this happen—and not just for the why-the-hell-do-boys-feel-the-need-to-do-this reason.

"Alright Tiny Dancer," Phil growled. "I bench more than you weigh, and you want to get up in my face? You think we all don't know that you scoot about on that stupid skateboard in an attempt to convince us that you're not some gay dancer boy?"

Now it was Nadia's turn to stand up. Lisa put her book down and grabbed Nadia's arm. "What did you just say?" Nadia snarled.

"Too easy," Phil laughed, brushing Nadia off with a wave of the hand before he turned back to Charlie. "I've seen you prancing about that place your mum has. If you're not gay, then I'm not this school's only chance at athletic success. And if I had to put up with that shrill harpy of a mother of yours, then I'd have gotten wasted and ploughed my car into a Jeep as well, just like your runaway dad."

My fists clenched under the table; I couldn't watch anymore. Maybe it was the lack of sleep. Maybe it was the two weeks of torment I'd suffered at the hands of some dead boy, this living boy, or the man who had buggered off to London with someone who wasn't my mum. But right then, I found my voice in all my pent-up frustration.

"Right, pencil-dick," I yelled as I stood up. My accent went full-on Glaswegian, the kind that you don't mess with. I'd probably been toning it down since I got here—now, was the time to crank it up to eleven. "Time to direct your anger at the right target for once."

Now I had his attention. I felt Lydia step up behind me, pushing some of her own sass and strength into me with the simple glare she was throwing his way.

I didn't lower my voice as I continued, "I don't know what my Mum has said to yours, but to be honest, that's not what you've got a problem with here, so let's stop pretending it is.

"From day one, you've been like human herpes. Irritating and hanging around without any sign of leaving. You looked at me and saw new-girl-equals-potential-target. And for a few days, you managed to keep me under your thumb, the way you like everyone in this damn school. But then I ignored you, met decent people, and managed to make my own space here and you just couldn't hack that. Had to make sure that I knew the pecking order. Well, guess what. I don't give a damn about your bloody playground hierarchy.

"So why don't you pretend like you've understood at least half of what I've just said and take your dumb jock arse and clear away from our table?"

Lydia leaned over and draped herself on my shoulder. "Jog on, pencil-dick," she sneered.

Everyone was watching, open-mouthed. Phil skimmed the room. At least five people had their phones out and were filming this. It would be on TikTok in less than twenty minutes.

"You've had it, Psycho House," he hissed, pointing at my face. "You've seriously had it."

But we'd won, and he stomped off.

Lydia gave my arm a squeeze and planted a dramatic kiss on my cheek. "Oh, kiddo," she said. "You're a legend now."

I flopped onto my seat, and the group swarmed around me with claps on the back and hair-ruffles. Charlie pulled a seat over and smiled sheepishly. Phil had burned him badly.

My hands were shaking. In fact, everything was shaking. Charlie put a hand on my arm, and I shook even more.

"You done good, kid," he said in a fake twenties' detective voice. A wink was thrown my way. The whole situation flashed before my eyes.

"Oh my God, what have I done?" I gushed.

"You were awesome." Lydia grinned. Apparently, I was now officially part of the gang and had passed the can-she-date-Charlie test. "But to hell with that, what's the deal with what's going on in your house? And can you come over tonight to tell me every little Psycho House detail?"

Him

I have to apologise for the cut on her arm. It was uncalled for, and I shouldn't have reacted like that. I know she understands me. She knows I won't do it again. But she's mad at me—of course she is.

I know what I need to do, and now, I finally have the means to do it. Now that I'm strong enough and I know all her passwords, I'm making her that playlist. Nothing says "I'm sorry for tearing your flesh open" like a playlist.

Well, I mixed CD with a hand drawn inset card would have been better but it's not the 2000s anymore, is it?

I used to make Stephanie apology CDs all the time. She loved them. She had a whole CD wallet full of them in her locker. I used to write on the blank discs in black and red felt tip pens – "Stephanie 4 Miles".

How stupid I was.

I login to Flora's Spotify and start to browse. I've been getting better at this while she's been out at school. I've even found new bands I like and new songs by ones I'd loved back when I was carrying an iPod Shuffle everywhere with me. Granted, I'm still definitely going to add in some of the songs I dreamt of burning onto a CD for her.

I hit the Create Playlist button, call it "For Flora" and start to drag songs into it.

"Second Chance" by Shinedown

"Leave Out All the Rest" by Linkin Park

"Burn" by The Cure

"Scarlet" by In This Moment

"My Heart is Broken" by Evanescence

"All Around Me" by Flyleaf

"End of Time" by Lacuna Coil

"Ever Dream" by Nightwish

"New Modern Love" by Halestorm

"Love Isn't Always Fair" by Black Veil Brides

"Where the Wild Roses Grow" by Nick Cave and the Bad Seeds

"Heart-Shaped Box" by Nirvana

I stop at a dozen songs. I spend quite a bit of time dragging them into the correct order and changing several tracks for other, better, more meaningful ones.

Emma Kathryn

She'll know how much I love her when she listens to this. I lie on her bed and let the playlist run from beginning to end. I imagine Flora doing the same, her hand pressed to her chest and tears forming in her eyes as she realises what she means to me.

This will do it. This will show her how real our love is.

Chapter Fifteen

Flora

You can imagine how elated my mum was when I texted her to say that I'd be going out that Friday night. Her response implied that she thought it was a date with Charlie. However, when I told her that it would be my new gal pal, it rapidly turned into a lesson about the importance of female friendships. Basically, she was just pleased that I wasn't turning into some kind of emotional hermit (as well as an actual hermit too, I guess).

Charlie and Lydia sat on either side of me on the floor as Nadia and Lisa came back in, brandishing three pizzas and a bag full of cans of juice. One pizza was just cheese, another was veggie, and the third was three different types of obscenely spicy meats. I opted for the cheese, but Lydia and Charlie both fired right into the spice.

"Okay," Lydia began, swallowing over a mouthful of solid heat. "Let's recap. A guy called Miles Allen died in your house, and now his stuff keeps turning up scary places."

"Killed himself," Lisa corrected, dipping the crust of her pizza into a blob of barbeque sauce she had squirted into the corner of the box. Nadia shook her head.

"I don't know how you can eat that stuff, it's rank rotten," she said.

"You're 100% wrong," Lisa replied. "BBQ sauce is life."

Given that we were living in the middle of nowhere, these pizzas were not Dominos, not Pizza Hut, not even Papa John's. Instead, they were from a chippy around the corner from Lydia's house. Weirdly enough, they tasted way better than any chain store pizza I'd ever had.

"Indeed," Lydia agreed. "Now this means that either some creep is sneaking into your house and trying to mess with you, or..." She paused for effect. Having now seen Lydia's inner sanctum, it was clear that she was absolutely loving this. "You've got a poltergeist."

"I don't think poltergeists are real," I said, trying to sound as sane as possible. "I mean, there has to be a sensible explanation here."

"Well, how likely is it that a stranger is moving things? Possible. How likely is it that someone has been writing secret notes to you in a phantom journal? Eh, maybe. How likely is it that someone is lurking behind you and whispering to you? Not even remotely."

I turned to Charlie, which probably wasn't sensible in front of his sister. "I'm not crazy, I promise," I whispered.

"Nobody thinks you're crazy," he said back, just as quietly. It was a little difficult to believe this. Absentmindedly, I scratched at the gash on my arm, which was still throbbing under the sleeve of my hoodie.

Lisa descended from her perch and joined us on the floor, placing the tablet down so we could all see it. A news report lay open. The picture of Miles used was the one from the school yearbook. "Alrighty, Miles Allen. Died aged seventeen. Suicide. Doesn't exactly say exactly how though. Seemed to have a girlfriend named Stephanie Jessel. Stephanie left school and went on to the University of Dundee, and is now a librarian in Inverness."

"Jesus, Lisa, you're such a stalker." Lydia laughed, giving Lisa a playful shove. "How did you even find the girlfriend stuff out?"

"Duh," Lisa groaned and flicked another tab open on the browser.

Facebook lay open, displaying the page for Stephanie Jessel. She looked almost exactly like she had in that World Book Day photograph, except older. She still had that goth thing about her, although it was a lot subtler now.

"Road trip tomorrow?" Lydia suggested.

I nearly choked on my pizza. "To where?" I coughed.

"Some library in Inverness?" she responded, as if it were the most obvious answer ever.

"Is that wise?" I asked.

"Only way to find answers now," Lisa said. "Research seems to be drawing a blank. And I personally don't think it's Phil. There's too much effort involved here."

"Plus, this is a guy who got the lead in the school play once and gave up because *There were too many words in it*," said Nadia. "It was *Grease*. Who doesn't already know all the songs in *Grease*?"

"You guys think it's definitely the ghost thing then?" I quizzed nervously. I so desperately just needed someone to say yes and that I wasn't going mad and imagining all the crap that was going on in my house. I needed someone to say "*Yes, he's moving your shit and picking fights between you and your mum.*"

"God, I hope so," Lydia beamed. "How exciting would that be?"

"Not for me! I've got to bloody well live with it."

Charlie gently placed a hand on my arm, and I realised I was still scratching. Instantly, I stopped. "How about we just rule it out to be sure then?" he said reasonably.

I nodded—it did seem like the sensible option. Relief hit me. Lydia was my shining light here. She believed me. Granted, this now validated my thoughts that there really was something horrible in my house.

"Unfortunately, I've got a study group tomorrow," Lisa said. "But I'll expect a full update, seeing as I'm the one who went and found Stephanie for you."

"Dork," Lydia jested.

"And I've got my running team," Nadia groaned.

"Looks like it's the Burns Squad, plus Flora," Lydia said with a smirk. "Oh my God, we can invite Lauren, my girlfriend."

"'She's from Inverness... you wouldn't know her'," everybody parroted.

"Very funny," Lydia groaned.

"I guess I can come," Charlie said with a smile.

"Don't you have ballroom lessons to assist in tomorrow?" Lydia interrogated him.

"Mum owes me a day off after I did an evening session during the week," he said.

Charlie and I glanced at one another. Even though we had been sending flirty songs all week, we hadn't actually spoken about the dancing thing. It felt like a secret that we shared—even though Lydia had watched the whole thing.

Lydia polished off the last insanely spicy slice. "Team Ghostbusters is officially me, Flora, and Charlie. Lisa and Nadia will get all the gossip on Monday. Lauren will meet us there. I've already texted her. But for now..." She leapt to her feet and opened her wardrobe door. All along the top shelf was a collection of DVDs. *"The Haunting, Thirteen Ghosts,* or *The Woman in Black?"*

Him

This is a bad sign. This morning, she's up early and something has her filled with nervous excitement. On top of that, she has been checking her phone obsessively. I don't like it. I don't like it at all. I fret as she buzzes around our bedroom.

Emma Kathryn

She tries on three different tops before settling for something with long floating sleeves. It has a V-neck with little laces tying it closed. Her black jeans hug her hips temptingly. I try to touch her a few times, but she moves like a hummingbird, constantly darting out of my reach.

The energy in the room feels like Stephanie the night before a big school dance.

Flora fills the air with perfume, dancing under the spray so that it lands delicately on her hair, her face, her body. I stand at her shoulder as she takes one last look in the mirror. She looks satisfied with her effort. If she was dressing like this for me, I'd think she was beautiful. But she's not, so she just looks like a slut, putting herself on display for someone else.

It's time for her to go. She pulls on her coat and grabs her bag. Then she sweeps out of the door, leaving me in a cloud of perfume. It smells disgusting now that she's no longer in the room, like formaldehyde on a corpse.

Chapter Sixteen

Flora

If she'd been excited at the prospect of me spending a Friday night with potential new friends, Mum was positively elated at the thought of me heading out with them for a whole Saturday. I was up early on Saturday morning and ready to catch the eleven o'clock bus to Inverness. Blairness didn't have a train station because, apparently, the industrial revolution never reached this tiny town.

Mum was also up nice and early and was reading *The Guardian* in the kitchen when I descended, fully dressed and ready to go. She had breakfast ready for me, but I was way too nervous. This was my first adventure with new friends, and I didn't want to screw it up. I was pretty lucky that they hadn't heard this whole ghost thing and run a mile.

I waited at the bus stop where we had agreed to meet. I had spent ages trying to work out what to wear that morning and had settled on black jeans, my creepers, a floaty *Archival Cycle* long-sleeved top that I'd found on Etsy, and my long coat since it was bloody freezing at this time of year. Somehow, through either sheer will or dark magic, I had managed to pull my hair half-up, half-down and make it look kind of nice. Mum had suggested a bit of makeup, and I gave her a rant about the expectations placed on young women to look good instead of being interesting or clever. Then I concluded that I might put a little mascara and lip-gloss on, but I did it after I left the house so as not to undermine my principles in front of Mum.

Being first at the bus stop was maybe a stupid move. I was afraid that it would seem overly keen or loser-ish, but I was also too afraid of missing the bus due to the long walk I had to make from my house into the village. Mum had offered to drive me, but I needed the walk to clear my head. Granted, I may have walked a little too fast. This meant a good ten minutes of standing on my own.

Luckily, the first person to appear was Charlie. He was wearing skinny jeans again and had a button-down shirt over a navy t-shirt. A thick hoodie covered both.

"Hey." He smiled and joined me in my casual leaning against the shoddy little rock wall that separated the pavement from yet another field – of which there are many in Blairness.

"Hey." I smiled back. We both had our hands pushed into our pockets and didn't say much for a little minute. It was a comfortable silence though. One that I was happy to spend an entire day wrapped up in. "No Lydia?"

"She was taking forever to get ready. She's all wound up about meeting Lauren."

"Ah. Girlfriend nerves. Totally understandable."

Suddenly though without the loud brashness of Lydia, I didn't know what to do with myself. I thought maybe she was starting to get under my skin. Not that that was a bad thing.

"I need to tell you something," he said, shattering the silence into a thousand tiny pieces. Oh God, here we go.

"Is it that this whole ghost thing is super stupid, because I'm starting to think that way too," I started to babble. I tried to fill the air with nonsense in the hope that he wouldn't be able to say something that would break my heart if I said it first. "Actually, I'm sorry that I've dragged you guys into this whole thing. It's ridiculous—"

"No," Charlie said, edging a little closer along the wall. "It's that I haven't stopped thinking about dancing with you all week."

My mouth fell open, but nothing came out. I wanted to say that I'd been thinking about it too, but I just said nothing. Words grew and formed in my throat, and I prepared to tell him I felt the same but instead, we were interrupted by a car horn as Lydia's mum stopped her tiny car in front of us. Lydia tumbled out of the car, and her mum sped off with a wave towards Charlie and me.

"Jesus, Charlie, you could have waited. I was only five minutes behind you," she gasped from bright purple lips.

She looked amazing. Her hair was wild but in an I-totally-meant-this-and-it-took-an-hour-to-do kind of way, and her eyes were decorated with thick eyeliner and silver eye shadow. She looked straight out of *The Craft*. For the first time since I'd met her, she had a piece of jewellery in every one of her piercings, not just in two or three of them. Her school docs had been replaced with black boots with rainbow laces and silver studs. Swung over her shoulder, she had a velvet bag with a tree of life embroidered on it. It was bursting with stuff.

Just like that, the moment was gone, and Lydia was bouncing about in front of us, listing off things she wanted to ask Stephanie Jessel when we got to the library. The three of us bundled on, and I ended up sitting next to Lydia—not Charlie, like I had been hoping for. I was happy to spend time with Lydia, even if she spent the first five minutes taking selfies to put on her Instagram and send to her mythical girlfriend, Lauren.

The bus took more than half an hour and stopped at around five other tiny towns that looked exactly like Blairness. At this time on a Saturday morning, we were the youngest people on the bus. The rest of the passengers were little old ladies, heading out to do their Marks and Spencer's shopping and weekly pilgrimages to their favourite tea room.

The countryside crawled by, and I watched as field became field became rocky hillside, before transforming into some misty woodland. The mist creeped me out. It looked as though there were a bunch of people in loose floaty dresses dancing amongst the trees. Having spent my life in the busy city of Glasgow, I'd never seen anything like this. When we got fog back in Glasgow, the weirdest thing you'd see looming out of it would be a bunch of drunk neds arguing over whose turn it was to buy the Buckfast. This was a million miles from what I was used to; it was like stepping into another world, the kind normally reserved for the fantasy books that I loved so much.

I wanted to get off the bus and walk into it. It was the kind of magical mist where faeries and sprites dwelled, known for stealing children, lost souls and shunned lovers. It was beautiful. My head burst with a thousand stories.

When we were about halfway there, Lydia dove into her bag and pulled something out. "Hey, I got you something," she said and held up her closed fist. It hid a surprise inside, and I immediately forgot about the wild landscape.

"You didn't need to get me anything!" I laughed.

"Shut it, or I won't give you it."

I mimed zipping my lips closed. Lydia descended on my jacket lapels and attached a small enamel pin. She looked proud of herself once it was attached.

I couldn't believe what it was. It was from the *Archival Cycle* —two crossed silver swords with a wisp of lilac smoke wrapping around them.

"You don't need to have all my blood to be my sister," Lydia quoted. "Or, well, any of it, in your case." It was a quote about Ophie and Faellah—the point where we discovered they're half-sisters. My heart melted.

"I absolutely love it," I told her. "Thank you so much."

"Yeah, yeah." Lydia shrugged. "Don't make a big deal out of it or anything."

But it was a big deal. It was a massive deal. I mattered to Lydia, and I was officially part of the gang. This proved it. I turned my head and beamed out of the window just as we arrived in Inverness, trying to hide my embarrassing levels of happy.

When we reached our stop, Lydia jumped out first. She was noticeably excited about this. I could only assume it was because she'd arranged to meet Lauren while we were here. She referred to a selection of questions she had typed up on the notes section of her phone. Without stopping to look around the city or get food or anything, we headed straight for the library. While I wanted to look around, having been desperate for city life for the last few weeks, I knew that wasn't what we were here for. My heart pounded in my chest, and I asked myself what the hell we thought we were doing.

Lydia strolled into the library as if she was researching a project for school, not trying to work out what had happened to the creep who was dripping stuff onto my bed and hiding things from me. As I stepped inside, I took a deep breath. Charlie took me by the arm and held me back for a moment.

"You don't have to do this if you don't want to," he told me.

"It's fine," I lied and gave him my best *"I'm okay really"* smile, the kind I give Mum when she asks if I've heard from Dad lately.

Charlie smiled back, but I couldn't help but wonder what he was thinking about all this. Lydia was getting a kick out of the weird element, but he didn't have any other reason to do this. Unless Lydia had talked him into it? I thought about what he said at the bus stop. Maybe he really was just here for me? But then he must be thinking I was some kind of madwoman who was imagining a ghost boy in her house. Surely that wasn't appealing.

We caught up with Lydia, who was waiting at the information desk. Someone was going to get Stephanie, it would seem. Then she appeared. Looking exactly like her Facebook picture, a young woman stood in front of us. She appeared to be very executive goth—long black hair, large, framed glasses, and a cardigan with a little Frankenstein's Monster embroidered onto the breast. Her smart black trousers were lined with green stitching to match her cardigan. I couldn't help but find her incredibly cool.

Lydia looked at her like she wanted to marry this woman. "I love her," Lydia whispered, eyes wide and filled with adoration.

"Hey guys," she smiled. "How can I help?"

Lydia took the reins, as she seems to do fairly often in this group. "Hi, we all go to Blairness High, and we were hoping that you could answer some questions that we have," she asked in her nicest talking-to-a-teacher voice.

"Oh, no way!" Stephanie laughed. "I went to Blairness High too!"

"That's pretty much why we're here," Lydia continued. From her bag of tricks, she produced a printed-out picture of Miles. "Would we be correct in saying that you knew this boy?" Lydia asked, sliding the picture over to Stephanie.

The polite librarian's face instantly fell. She looked as if she had just seen Jack the Ripper. "Sorry, but what are you guys doing here?" she asked with a tremble in her voice.

"We just want to know what happened to him," Lydia said, trying to speak calmly. "And what kind of trouble he may have caused." Charlie and I hung back a little and let her do all of the talking.

I kept asking myself why I was here and what I was thinking. My arm still hurt. In fact, it has probably hurt more since we had stepped into the library. I wrapped my hand around where it pulsed under my coat and did my best not to let anyone know that it was bothering me again.

"I think you should go," Stephanie said. She made as if to leave the desk.

"He's back," Lydia said, dropping her nice act and now speaking sternly. "He's back, and he's harassing my friend."

Stephanie looked helplessly at us. I stayed back. "That can't be," Stephanie said. Behind her glasses, her eyes went wide. "He's dead. I saw him. I know he's dead."

"How did he die?" Lydia asked, ready for every grizzly detail.

Stephanie looked very pale—paler than her pale foundation was already making her appear. It was as if she really had seen a ghost. "I don't know if I can do this. Look, kids, I'm at work. I should be getting back to what I was doing..."

"My friend can't sleep," Lydia continued. She had worked out that I wasn't willing to come forward on this one and seemed quite content with taking the lead. To be honest, I was quite happy to let her do so. There was also something intensely comforting about hearing her call me *"friend."* "He's messing with her head and invading her home. And I can't help but feel like you know this already."

"He's dead," Stephanie repeated.

"Hey, nobody's arguing that point," Lydia replied. "All we want to know is how he died so we can try to put a stop to all the weird crap that's going on in her house."

There was a beat between Lydia and Stephanie. Coldness washed over me, and I swear I could feel Miles at my shoulder, breathing into my ear.

"If I tell you how he died, do you promise to leave?" Stephanie asked, looking a little more than just distressed now. We all nodded.

"He went into the bath and tried to slit his wrists. He only managed one, but it was enough. I saw him. I had gone around to the house to tell his mum what he was planning, but I was too late. I'd even phoned the house, but no one answered."

"Did he tell you he was going to do this?" Lydia asked.

"He'd planned it in great detail," she sighed. "He decided that I was supposed to be a part of it. I kept telling him no, and that it was ridiculous and awful and insane. But he didn't care. He'd decided that if I was going to leave him, he couldn't live without me. And I'd be so miserable, he was sure I'd follow shortly after him. This was what I had to listen to every day."

I didn't doubt that for a second.

"You were trying to leave him?" Lydia pressed.

"I'd been trying to leave him for months, but he kept sucking me back in. Then, I got accepted into uni, and it was the perfect opportunity for escape. But that was when the threats started. Miles Allen was the kind of cruel person that wouldn't just threaten to harm himself if I left, but also threatened to hurt me and everyone I cared about. But I swear, that's all I thought they were—just words to frighten me. I never really thought he'd go through with it."

The words started to pour out of Stephanie. This information seemed like something she kept close to the chest. Perhaps this was something she only ever told one or two people she let get close enough to see the cracks in her solid gothic demeanour. But we had the privilege of being strangers, people she could tell with little to no repercussions for her. She continued, "He demanded to be around me every waking second of the day but would talk to me like he didn't give a damn about me. Once he asked me to throw myself in front of a bus so that when they were scraping me off the pavement, if someone asked if he knew me, he could say I meant nothing to him."

My hands started to sweat. I'd seen something like that in one of the notebooks. I knew that she was speaking his words verbatim. It was like she was reading it straight off of one of the pages. As if it had fluttered through the library door and landed in front of her. I started to feel sick.

Whispers started in my ear. I only caught the occasional word, but they weren't pleasant.

"He had decided that we were better than everyone around us. No, not us. *He* was better. I was just an accessory. He decided we were going to be together forever, in life *and* death. Kept spouting all this *Romeo and Juliet* nonsense. When my university acceptance arrived, that was my wake-up call. It should have been months before that, but he was so damn charming. I told him I'd been accepted, and I was leaving him. There was no changing my mind. I wanted to leave Blairness, and that meant leaving him. He said if I left him, he'd kill himself for real this time.

"But I couldn't let him do it because I wasn't the kind of monster that could have this information and not do something with it. And anyway, at the time, I was convinced that we were in love. I didn't want him to die.

"So, I called his house. Repeatedly. I got no answer. Eventually, I went around to stop him and...things got crazy. He ended up dead on the bathroom floor and I was a broken person. I don't think he meant to die. Maybe he just wanted to see what I'd do. If I'd try to save him. Ultimately, I think he meant to scare me. And he fucking did.

"That's it. That's the whole story and that's everything you're getting."

I'd spent this entire story staring at the floor. I wasn't sure I could bear the pain on her face. Once she'd almost finished, I looked up and she was looking straight at me.

She knew.

"Let me see it," she ordered me. The entire group turned around and looked at me with the same confused faces.

Without a word, I stepped forward and pulled my sleeve up. The wound on my arm was worse than the day I'd done it. The tear was wide and pulsing. Something seeped around the edges, and my entire forearm hurt if I touched it. I heard Stephanie hiss. I'm not sure what was exchanged between Lydia and Charlie, but something silent went on between them.

Stephanie reached across the desk and took my sore wrist with her left arm. She pulled up the edge of her own left sleeve to reveal an old pink scar. "Exactly a year after he died, I'd come back home for the summer, and I had an accident with an old picture I found of us. The frame broke, and I cut myself on the glass. I didn't even know that I had any pictures left of the two of us. It didn't heal until months later when I left to start my second year of uni. Maybe that sacrificial burn-everything-that-reminds-me-of-school bonfire might have helped too. Who knows? Nothing heals the soul like destroying everything your ex has ever touched."

"What am I supposed to do?" I whispered, tears filling my eyes.

"The only thing that stopped him from hurting me was dying," she said with a shrug. "I don't think I can help. I've spent a lot of time and energy putting that behind me. I'm sure you'll forgive me if I say that this is the most that I'm willing to do."

This wasn't good enough for Lydia. She was not one for admitting defeat.

"This girl lives in his old house," she said. "She's putting up with this crap twenty-four-seven."

"I'm sorry, but I'm done here."

Stephanie started to gather some books from a trolley behind her. Moving away was a pretty clear signal that this chat was complete, but Lydia didn't care.

"I think you're missing the part where she gets harassed in the house he died in," Lydia yelled over the desk.

From somewhere in the library, someone shushed Lydia. A flash of disgust flickered over her face.

"Oh, bugger off," Lydia said in the direction of the shusher. "See the state of her arm? Why would you want her to go through what you did?"

A man appeared at Lydia's side. While he wasn't quite what I expected from a bouncer, he was exactly what I expected from library security—tall, but not exactly burly. Bulkier more than anything. He said something to Lydia in a very low, very calm voice, and then Charlie had her by the arm and was leading her outside.

Feet rooted to the spot, I stood there in the middle of the library, staring at the woman who had suffered before me. I thought about her scar and about the things he said to her and about the fact that she had to leave for it all to stop. Tears pricked at my eyes and my breathing threatened to escalate. Stephanie looked up and held my gaze, mouth open, as if she wanted to say something. As quickly as she had started, she gave up and walked out of sight.

Around me, the few people who were attending the library stared at me. Two women whispered. I yanked my sleeve down further than I had to. Then, I left the library.

Outside, Charlie and Lydia were arguing. Well, not really arguing. Lydia was shouting and rambling and every now and then Charlie got half a sentence in before Lydia ran away with his idea and claimed it as her own. I sat down on the library steps and put my head in my hands.

Pressing my palms against my forehead meant I could feel the pulse from my left arm thump right through my skull. I felt a tiny bit sick. That could've been nerves though. I tried to decide whether I was mad at Stephanie or not. Probably not. If I'd gotten away from Miles, I wouldn't be in much of a hurry to go back either.

Someone sat down next to me and pulled me into a slightly unwelcome hug. It crushed my sore arm and pulled me out of my funk, which quite frankly I was nowhere near ready to leave. Lydia's arms enveloped me.

"Sorry, petal," she sighed into my hair.

This was a closer hug than I'd shared with any of my friends, and I desperately wanted to push her off. However, I didn't. I fell into Lydia's hug, and I cried. She stroked my hair and whispered nice things to me. She told me "I got you" and "It'll be okay", and I believed them like they were truths.

Charlie kept his distance. I watched him as he paced the edge of the pavement, balancing only half of his foot on the kerb. It looked like someone had photoshopped out his skateboard from under his feet.

"That was a bust," Lydia groaned. She leaned back and brushed down where she'd messed up my hair. Now that I was paying proper attention, I realised how full-on goth she was out of her school uniform. Her eye makeup was amazing. In fact, she looked as though she was auditioning for a gender-bent version of *The Crow*.

"No, it wasn't," I said, gently shrugging her off but making it seem like I was fixing my hoodie. "It mostly tells me I'm not crazy."

"Nobody thought you were crazy," Lydia said. She tried to smile but her face was still flushed like she was angry. "Just a little weird. But that's okay. We like weird here."

Chapter Seventeen

Flora

The next thing I knew, we were all sitting in a quaint little café with a hot chocolate in front of me. Lydia was sitting next to me and had apparently adopted the mantle of my new protector. She kept looking at the door though. Charlie was across from me. He nonchalantly sipped on a cup of coffee (one he had watered down to hell with an insane amount of sugar and milk) while Lydia chewed on her nails as she waited.

Apparently, this was confession part two: the pair wanted to know about my arm. I told them about the box doing its reappearing act and cutting myself on the aftershave bottle.

"See!" Lydia burst when I finished. "I told you all she was the real deal! That bottle was broken in the bin! How could someone find all the bits and transfer all the box contents back upstairs?! HOW?!"

Something sharp panged in my chest. Lydia's words made me realise that there had been a conversation about the authenticity of my claims, and Lydia had possibly been the only one on my side.

"But seriously," she added, swinging back around to me, "you need to get that arm checked out now. That is beyond infected."

I nodded and slid my arm under the table. I rested my hand on my knee, safely out of sight. Lydia continued to champion my tale and babbled about how she'd always believed in ghosts, especially after that time with her great aunt who was dead...

She stopped mid-sentence. "Ohmygod," she muttered all in one breath.

Leaping to her feet, she rushed towards the door and threw her arms around a girl who had just walked in.

"I'm guessing that would be Lauren," Charlie said.

Lydia hugged the girl hard, and they kissed in a way that was both passionate and a little nervous. It was as if they were still working out how to do it. It was all ridiculously cute.

Lauren was not even remotely what I imagined of Lydia's imaginary girlfriend. I think I pictured another extra from *Interview with the Vampire*. Instead, she had long tousled fair hair and a wide, warm smile. She wore a baggy flannel shirt over a band t-shirt, and she was in printed leggings, ending with faux-fur-topped boots. A denim jacket topped it all off, and a bag covered with pins and badges fell to the ground as she hugged her girlfriend.

Lydia dragged the newcomer over as we cleared enough space so they could sit together.

"Gang," she announced with pride, "this is Lauren. By the way, she's an *Archival Cycle* virgin, but try not to let that shape your judgement on her in any way."

"You're such a dork," Lauren laughed before kissing her girlfriend again.

The table burst with talking and laughing; everyone wanted to know more about the new girl. Charlie moved to let the pair sit next to each other and sidled in beside me. Lauren looked only mildly overwhelmed, and it was quite clear that this was the first time she was meeting any of Lydia's friends. Lydia kept darting her eyes my way as if searching for approval. I nodded every time she looked at me. This was evidently a big step for her.

Rocking my leg back and forth, I accidentally brushed Charlie's knee. I yanked my hand back as if I had been electrocuted. He looked up from his coffee. I must have looked unbelievably guilty and glanced at Lauren and Lydia. They were both preoccupied with their own chatter. Glancing back at Charlie, he winked. I smiled and returned my knee to its original position. This time he bumped me.

Our smiles widened.

"Welcome to the Ghostbusters, Lauren," Charlie joked, and everyone started to giggle.

This was the happiest I'd been in months. Maybe even in years.

"Thanks," Lauren beamed and slid her fingers through Lydia's. "I've heard loads about all of you."

"Not gonna lie," Charlie said. "For a little while, none of us thought you were real."

"Whatttttt?!" Lydia burst.

"I mean, you did keep saying 'You wouldn't know her, she doesn't go here,'" I agreed. It was true. It had definitely fluttered through my head that Lauren wasn't real and just a way to fend off the homophobes and nosy folk at school.

"I can totally see you doing that," Lauren told Lydia, and they smiled in a way that showed how much they liked each other. It was also clear that they had both started to relax a bit now that the friend meet-up had gone well.

"Right, Flora, gimme your phone," Lydia said, tearing her hands off Lauren long enough to swipe my phone away from me.

"Hey!" I protested, attempting to grab it back.

"Relax, I'm doing something good. Now, what's your passcode?"

I refused to tell her, and she spent a moment staring at me and tapping on the table, thinking up combinations of four numbers. An imaginary lightbulb when off over her head, and she swiftly tapped in a combination.

The right combination.

"How?!" I squealed, as everyone around me made noises of surprise.

"6425—the code for the vault in the second *Archival* book. The sixth of April and the second of May. Ophie and Faellah's birthdays. So predictable, missus."

"I hate you," I groaned, wishing we hadn't talked about the whole secret sister plot over WhatsApp last week.

"No, you don't." She smiled, showing those bright teeth under all that purple lipstick that had inexplicably survived all the kissing.

"I need to come up with a new passcode now."

"1234 has always worked for me," Charlie, the tech guru, joked.

Lydia went to the camera app and began an impromptu photo shoot. "What are you doing?" I asked. Obediently, I grinned when she pulled me in for a hugging selfie.

"We're letting the world see how much of a good time you're having here with us mad Northerners. Showing them all you're #blessed."

"None of us would ever say #blessed."

"Pffft, that's old Glaswegian Flora talking. Mad Highland Flora says whatever the hell she wants."

As Lydia's thumbs went to town on my Instagram and Twitter accounts, Lauren leaned forward. "Do you miss Glasgow?" she asked, totally oblivious to any rant I'd had with Lydia on this.

"I think if you'd asked me that two weeks ago, the instant answer would have been yes," I told her. "But it's changing. I mean yeah, I still miss my old bedroom, and it does still sting that I had a whole life and it's just gone now. And maybe I miss being able to get into the city centre in seven minutes and going to the cinema whenever I got the urge. But this place is different. Maybe it'll be totally different once there's not a psycho keeping me awake at night. But for now, I think Blairness is starting to grow on me. Plus, I guess the locals are alright."

The table of new friends all grinned at me as Lydia passed my phone back.

"Let the *Weegies* fill with jealous rage," she cackled before wrapping her arm around Lauren again.

Tapping through my Instagram story, I saw a life filled with promise. Pictures of Lydia and Lauren, Charlie pulling a face, hot chocolate mugs nearly finished, the group all grinning like mad. My favourite was the one of Lydia and me with our cheeks practically pressed together. I know that Lydia had put these up to make my old friends, my ex, and even my dad realise that I didn't need them (and reassure my stalker mother that I'm doing okay), but nothing in it was lies. I looked happy because I was happy. We all looked like friends on a trip out because we really were friends.

For the second time today, I felt like crying. Just for very different reasons this time.

Lydia banged on the table and grasped the attention of all of us. "That's it," she announced. "We're having a seance."

"No, we're not," I grumbled.

"We are," Lydia refuted. "I'm practically a Mesmer. I'll conduct it."

"No, you will not," Lauren bounced back. "And you are not a Mesmer. This isn't Victorian London, you know."

"I've got way more style than those prissy old crones," she grumbled. "Anyway, I mean it. I reckon we all go round to Flora's house, sit in the dark, and collectively tell Miles to bugger off."

"Lydia," Lauren moaned and put down her phone now that she'd saved everyone's numbers and we'd all swapped socials. "You don't know the first thing about holding a seance."

An unmistakable look of disgust fluttered over Lydia's face. She was not one for standing aside and letting others take the lead. I panicked and wondered what Lydia had in store for her planned seance and supposed mesmerism.

"Alright," she said, scraping at the last of her food. "I'll make a deal with you. We'll all go away today and come up with a Save Flora plan, and then we'll decide what's to be done on Monday at Writers Group, and I'll call you immediately after. That sound like an acceptable plan, Miss Worrybutt?"

A sly smile spread across Lauren's mouth. "Seems a fair deal to me."

All through this, Charlie and I had been swapping knowing glances. I thought about his words that morning. He said he'd been thinking about dancing with me. I'd never had anyone talk like this to me before.

In my old school, I'd had two romantic encounters. There was my ex, who I was done thinking about, but there had been a nearly sort-of boyfriend before him. I'd kissed a boy called Aaron Abernathy a handful of times, but neither of us were really into the other one. It was more that primal call when you just want to know what another person feels like, what they taste like, what they smell like up close. Instead, it had been a couple of clumsy kisses with a guy who only used his PlayStation for playing *FIFA* on. I tried to actually spend time with him once by suggesting we try out the new *Tomb Raider* reboot. He knocked me back in favour of playing online footy with his headset on so that he could scream obscenities at his poor opponent who probably just wanted a quiet game after a long day at work. *FIFA, FIFA, FIFA.* That was it. Honestly, it's like having a sports car and only ever using it to do doughnuts in an Asda car park.

As for Dani, I'd thought that had been real. But I also thought that my friends had been real too. Dani and I hung about with the drama squad. We all did everything together, and I thought I was the queen bee there. We all got pizza, we all went to the pictures, we all went round someone's house and drank vodka with jelly babies dropped in the bottle because someone's sister had told us that it was easier to drink that way. Dani and I made sense. We became a couple. That was that. Then I left. And then Dani and Lucy made sense. I was forgotten.

This was different. Being around Charlie was like there was electricity charging all through my body. It was exciting and scary, but scary in a good way—not like the fear I felt in that house. To be honest and perhaps a little cold, being around Charlie was a welcome distraction. Spending the day out in the city was also an excellent way to get out of the house and pretend like I wasn't going back to my own dead stalker.

There was something incredibly flippant about the way everyone joked about my ghost and the excitement Lydia was getting from this. The important fact of the matter was that these people weren't having to live with this. They could both go home to their own quiet, warm beds. No one was going to be whispering in their ears all night. They wouldn't be getting subjected to blasts of cold air across their faces. And absolutely nothing evil was sitting in a box directly above their heads.

§⚫

We spent a good chunk of the afternoon wandering around the shops of Inverness. We went into stores and joked about music and films.

It became clear though that Lydia and Lauren both wanted and needed some alone time. Living in different towns and communicating almost entirely online meant that moments like this were a rarity.

"So, uh," Lydia began, suddenly more nervous than I'd ever seen her, "I think we're going to hit the cinema. See that new slasher movie. *The Lonely Hearts Killer*. You know, the one where the serial killer hunts down couples but then *only kills the guys!*"

"Oh man," I said, giving Charlie a gentle elbow and a wink. "I hate horror movies."

"Yeah," Charlie agreed, nodding overenthusiastically. "They're the worst. All that blood, death, and bad acting."

"And that one sounds particularly scary," I agreed.

"All that feminism, too—killing only the guys." Charlie nodded. "And you know they'll end up making like four sequels. If I see this one, I'll need to see them all."

Lauren was blushing and smiling widely. Charlie and I were truly the bad actors, but our point was made loud and clear. Lydia mouthed, *thank you*, with her eyes filled with gratitude.

"Well, I guess we better get going or we'll miss the start," Lydia said. She and Lauren took hands. I could practically feel the fireworks. "Can't miss the first teenage boy being gutted from neck to navel."

"You're so weird," Lauren said. Even more chemistry flickered between them.

After a round of "it was nice to meet you" and hugs from Lydia, they were gone. Charlie and I looked at one another. What now?

"You wanna go for a walk?" Charlie asked. I did.

"I just want to clear something up first," I said. "I freaking love horror movies."

"Oh, me too, but Lydia is scarier than anything Freddy Krueger could ever do to me."

"Plus, we literally just watched *Thirteen Ghosts* with her last night."

"That, too."

On what was a very cold February afternoon, Charlie and I walked a path along the side of the river, taking the longest route imaginable to where our bus stop stood. The wind was brisk and there were only a few people around on the walk we took together. I felt elated and anxious as we walked side by side, each too nervous to say very much. Again and again, we looked up and smiled.

Eventually, we crossed the river and started to head back towards where we'd already walked past the bus stop. As we crossed over the water, I stopped. Charlie turned around to see what was wrong.

"What are we doing?" I asked, shrugging my shoulders as the water rushed under us.

"Going home, I guess?" Charlie hazarded. He sauntered back towards me, hands in the pockets of his jeans. This seemed quite a feat considering the fact that these were skinny jeans he was wearing.

"Yeah, I don't mean like walking or tormenting girls in libraries or planning some kind of mad ghost hunt in my house."

"Whatever do you mean?" he asked playfully, showing that he totally knew what I meant.

"You're trying to make me say it, aren't you?" I joked.

"I most certainly am." He smiled.

I took a deep breath and attempted to pick up where we left off. "You said that you've been thinking about that dance," I said, my voice broken by a nervous wobble.

Charlie shifted his feet, losing his cool for only a moment before returning to jokes and sass. "That's because your salsa skills need some real work," he lied, leaning against the railing of the bridge we stood on. Water ran gently under our feet, carrying dead leaves and twigs.

The joking was making things way easier. I relaxed a little and leaned against the bridge next to him. "That was because I had a poor teacher," I informed him.

Charlie scoffed. "I'll have you know that your - very gifted - salsa teacher has been dancing since he could walk - whether he liked it or not, I may add - and if you couldn't dance then it certainly was not his fault."

"Oh really?"

"Really."

"Then what do you suggest?"

"I'd suggest that maybe, if you'd like to, we could continue to try dancing together and see how that goes?" he asked.

Don't grin, Flora, I begged myself. *Please don't grin and ruin what is quite possibly the coolest conversation you've ever had in your life.* I tried to maintain my composure and looked him straight in the eye.

"I'd like that," I told him. "I'd like that a lot."

On the way home, we sat beside one another and laughed more than I had in weeks. Our laughter rang out through the bus (which was much busier than it had been this morning), which got us several disgruntled looks.

Charlie told me about his parents. Almost all of his stories involved some kind of dancing. He told me about the time he got detention for telling a drama teacher that they were trying to teach a class how to waltz wrong for a play. Even though no one had to waltz at all, they just had to look like they were dancing a bit for some kind of Jane Austen-style school play. He told me about all the ceilidhs his mother used to love going to once she and his father moved here. In his first year at high school, Charlie nearly got a kicking from Phil and his squad for being the only person in his class to enjoy doing social dancing in PE at Christmastime. He also discovered that I'd never seen a film called *Take the Lead* in which Antonio Banderas teaches inner-city teens self-respect through dance. Apparently, it was his mother's favourite film, and he had pretty much decided that the next time my mum dumped me for a dance class, we were watching it. Because it would seem that if he had been subjected to it as many times as his mother made him watch it, then I deserved to suffer it at least once. It would seem that his mother considered Antonio Banderas and Enrique Iglesias to be interchangeable when it came to describing Spanish men as national treasures.

At one point though, as the laughter cooled to giggling, he went a little sombre and told me, "You know what Phil said about my dad isn't true."

"I know," I told him, unsure whether I did or not. Maybe it didn't really matter though. I had enough family drama without judging his.

When it was my turn, I told him about Mum's books, and all the times she would take me along on her exciting book tours. Dad never came, but I used to love going with her. Granted, I hated the signing bits. Hours and hours of Mum signing books for queues of people. I would usually go hide behind some bookshelves and read something scary instead. I told him about my favourite books and about how I discovered the *Archival Cycle* at a book festival with Mum. Since we were allowed to get serious after his little interlude about his dad, I told Charlie about mine. I told him that Dad was off in London, turning my favourite story into something else while managing to totally avoid all contact with me. Telling so many stories about Mum and how she encouraged me to love books also made me realise how little Dad was there. It bothered me that I'd still been checking up *Archival* news online in the hope that even just his name would surface somewhere.

I told Charlie this, and he looked like he understood. I know that he probably didn't, but it was nice that he was trying. Not once did he tell me that it was cool that Dad was adapting what were unmistakably his favourite books. Instead, he just listened and let me rant.

After being disgustingly honest about some stuff, we hit a happy little quiet moment. The bus wasn't far from Blairness now and we didn't have much longer to sit next to each other. Smiles and glances got all sparky again and I realised that we were sitting right against each other now. We must have been accidentally moving closer and closer together throughout the journey.

"Hey," he said softly.

"Hey," I replied with a smile.

"Can I be bold?" he asked, looking more nervous than he had all day.

"Oh, I dunno," I said, not overly sure what he was about to do. I felt myself tense a little. What would I class as bold? "Depends on how bold we're talking here."

"Could I put my arm around you?" he queried awkwardly, suddenly looking way younger than his sixteen years.

Good god, this boy was adorable.

"Yes please," I answered with a wild smile that I just couldn't subdue anymore.

Charlie reached his arm out over the back of the bus seats and rested a hand on my shoulder. Very gently, he pulled me closer until we were sitting in a comfortable half hug. I leaned in against him, my other shoulder nestling in under his outstretched arms.

We sat like that for the rest of the trip and continued our chat about bad family films we'd been forced to watch over the years. I felt safe.

When we reached our stop, we got off the bus. As a habit, I always thanked the driver and Charlie followed suit. We stepped off and onto the opposite pavement as we started and, at last, we had come full circle. By now it was getting dark, and Charlie offered to walk me home. The independent woman in me wanted to make a clever remark about how I'd managed to walk here all by myself this morning, but I quite wanted to spend a little more time with him. So, I negotiated that he could walk with me part of the way. He seemed happy with this, and we walked most of the way until we reached that bloody pond with the little island in the middle.

We stood for a moment, listening to the quiet quacking of the ducks settling down for the evening. The arm around me had transformed into a little handholding and that was how we were at this very moment.

"I should be getting home." I sighed, holding his hand even tighter. Common sense told me that I'd be seeing him on Monday. It would only be a full day when I wouldn't see him. But now that we'd touched it felt like a huge Charlie-less void.

"Yeah," he agreed, stroking his thumb against the side of my hand. It was the single nicest sensation I'd ever experienced. I might have been hyperbolising a little. But it was pretty damn yummy anyway.

In the distance, a single duck quacked louder than all the others.

"Even that duck agrees," Charlie added, making me laugh and ruining the little feeling of sadness I was experiencing with the thought of leaving him.

Inwardly I told myself off for being so sappy, but all of my hard edges were starting to soften. At the same time, the sappy side tried to reason with the hard side. Maybe it wasn't so bad to feel like this. Maybe it was okay to let someone in now and again.

And I really wanted it to be Charlie.

"Hey," I said.

"Hey," he replied.

"Can I be bold?"

"Oh, I dunno," he said with a grin. "Depends on how bold we're talking here."

I grinned and leaned in a little. Not too much to be presumptuous but just enough to make clear what I was about to say.

"Could I kiss you?" I asked so softly that I was practically whispering.

I knew what the answer was. He was already leaning in before he spoke. I waited for him to say it anyway.

"Yes please," he whispered back.

Our first kiss was soft and tender and filled with warmth against the northern chill. Heart beating like a hummingbird, I pulled him close, and he returned the favour. I couldn't get over how soft his lips were. A tiny little strip of stubble crawled up his jaw and occasionally tickled my skin. He smelt amazing. Coconut shampoo, it had to be.

It made me want to run my hands through his hair, but I thought that would be a little much for the first kiss. Silently I cursed my mother for subjecting me to romance novels from such a young age.

No one could be seen for miles and the only witness to our moment was the wildlife. His breath was hot against my face when we came up for air. He let out a little sigh and this made me smile so wide that I flashed teeth.

"Man, I'm so glad you suggested that because I've been trying to work up the courage to do it since Lydia and Lauren left," he said with his breath still all erratic and excited.

Seriously, this boy was adorable.

"I'm glad you agreed to it." I smiled back, pressing my forehead against his.

"Oh, I would've agreed to it in a heartbeat," he said, and I felt his mouth close to mine again.

Oh boy, was I falling hard.

"Wanna go for it again then?" I chanced my arm by asking for round two.

This time, he didn't even say yes, and he went in for the kiss. There was more fire this time. We'd both tested the waters and they were just to our liking. Now we wanted to swim deep. I went for the hair manoeuvre, and he moaned a little against my mouth. This was heavenly.

So far removed was it from my previous awkward fumbles, this felt like being kissed for the first time. It felt like the imaginary kisses you see in films or read about in books—the kind that never involves clashed teeth or strings of saliva or banging noses. Instead, it was just right.

We separated but stayed close. His hands were on my waist and mine rested on his upper arms. I didn't want to let go but it was getting darker and that made the trip home more treacherous. I considered letting him walk me the whole way home, but I thought of having to deal with Mum at the front door. Worse still, she'd try to invite him inside and insist that he had dinner with us. So, I had to be the one to ruin the moment.

"I really should get home now," I told him with regret.

"Yeah, same." Charlie sighed, pulling me in for a last hug. "You know that we're both probably got about forty messages from Lydia already, right?"

Lydia. I felt like I was betraying a rule of sisterhood by kissing her brother. I'd need to come up with a way to fix that—and quickly.

I laughed. "I'll have to brace myself for that. Do you want to tell anyone yet?" It had to be asked.

"I think I'd rather we decide what we want to do first," he said, and I totally agreed.

"What do you want to do?"

"I kind of just want to kiss you all night and then talk about the *Archival* books and then kiss you some more and then come up for enough air to eat pizza."

We both giggled, and it resulted in a series of shorter, sweeter kisses. Pecks, really. Still nice though.

"Well, that's not really an option tonight, but how about we both go home, and chat over the weekend? See how we feel once the endorphins start to fade?" I suggested, letting go long enough to regret it and reach for his hand again.

"I don't see this fading for a while," he said while playing with my fingers.

He glanced up at the sky and then at his watch. It was getting dark now and I couldn't risk staying any longer. Not with that stupid lakeside trail to take. We both knew this date (was it even a date?) was over.

"Okay," he eventually said. "You know that Lydia has probably psychically picked up on this, right? I mean, she has some all-seeing-eye shit and will see right through me."

"Yeah, I totally didn't mean Lydia when I was asking who we should tell. I felt she was a given." I laughed.

"Bloody Lydia." He sighed and rolled his eyes. Our hands detached. "Safe trip home."

"Yeah." I nodded. "You could text me when you get in. Just let me know that you got home, okay?"

He nodded with a little more enthusiasm than was necessary for a checking-in message. Although, we both knew that it was going to be more than a checking-in message. It was probably going to involve staying up all night talking.

Swiftly, before I knew what was happening, he pulled me in for one last goodbye kiss. It was equally amazing, and I didn't even mind the surprise. Breathless and light-headed, we said our goodbyes, and both began to walk in opposite directions.

Even though I knew that I should keep my cool and not do what I was about to, I looked back twice. And I caught him doing the same on the second glance.

However, once I turned back on the second glance, I imagined that I saw a black figure standing in the middle of the pond's island. There was no way there could be. It must have been a trick of the encroaching night shadows, but it really looked like there was a tall, slim figure watching our goodbye. I shook my head and looked again but on the double-take, it was gone.

Now filled with an uncomfortable mixture of nerves, excitement, and fear, I dropped Mum a text that I was off the bus and on the way home. Could she meet me part of the walk down? Almost instantly, she replied in the affirmative.

I flicked on the little torch (in the shape of Navi from the *Legend of Zelda* games) that I had hanging from my keys and walked as quickly as I could towards the house. Mum met me barely five minutes after my text, and we walked up the rest of the way together. She'd left the porch light on so that we had a beacon to light our way home. As I stepped into the glow, Mum stopped me and looked at me carefully. Suddenly her face lit up and she gave me a hug, right where we stood on the house porch.

"What?!" I yelled and tried to shrug her off.

"You've got the look of a girl who just kissed a boy she likes for the first time," Mum announced and unlocked the front door.

I felt the fire of a thousand suns rising in my cheeks. "Ohmygod Muuuuum," I whined and rushed inside.

"And now I know it's true," she chuckled. She chased me for another hug once we were both safely inside and with the door locked behind us.

Him

The rage is unbearable. How fucking dare she?

She was out there kissing some guy while I was waiting here for her like an idiot. A day and a half she's been away from me. It's goddam outrageous. I want to wring her beautiful neck. I want to see her suffer. I want to show her what she's done to me.

I stand behind her as she steps into the back garden with her mobile phone in hand. She scrolls through her contacts—a list of people I don't know and who she's probably been laughing about me with. With slight hesitation, she taps the name Lydia and I see her exhale deeply as it rings. I move closer, practically pressing my body against hers so I can hear the call. This is the one. The friend who's been keeping her away. I hate her.

Absent-mindedly, she scratches at the wound on her arm. It looks stunning in the dark of the garden. There's a faint smell of rot coming from her which she's attempted to cover up with sickly sweet perfume. I desperately want to touch it. She winces and takes her hand away from it, as if realising she's been picking the edges.

A voice on the other end answers. "What's up, witch?"

"I'm so sorry, am I interrupting anything?" Flora asks, now fidgeting with the zip on her coat.

"Nah, the film's just finished and I'm waiting for Lauren to come out of the bathroom. What do you think? Do you like her? Isn't she great?"

"She's genuinely amazing. Well done, you."

"Thanks. This isn't the debrief you're calling for, is it?"

"No. Actually..." Flora begins.

I want to hear her say it. Tell her you're a whore. Watch her hate you and tell her never to call you again.

"I have a confession."

I say actual words this time. I snarl it in the ear that doesn't have the phone pressed against it. I'm so close I could bite her neck. I want to bite her and rip and taste her flesh and hurt her.

She will hate you, *I hiss.* You have betrayed her. You have betrayed me. You deserve to be hated by everyone you care about.

"I kissed Charlie. I mean, we kissed. He was very much a willing participant. And I'm sorry and I don't know if I should have but I wanted to tell you anyway. I'm sorry."

The tin voice on the other end of the phone doesn't sound angry though. It laughs. And not a cynical laugh. "Okay, two things. No, wait. Make it three," the disembodied voice of Lydia begins.

"One: I know. Charlie texted me almost immediately. Something about it being like when Ophie and Freiten finally kissed at the end of Archival Book One. Two: I'm happy for you. You deserve it. You've pretty much been miserable since you got here, and I've seen you smile more today than the entire time I've known you. And three: My brother is a grown-ass person. He can make his own decisions, and so can you. Neither of you owes me anything. You got that?"

"Sure." Flora laughs. Her face is positively red and beaming. She looks ugly like this. "Thank you, Lydia."

"Yeah yeah, I'm the best. Now bugger off and let me get my own snogging time."

"Okay! Bye. Text me later."

"Obviously."

The phone goes dead, and Flora lets out a deep sigh of relief. I am frozen on the spot, getting madder and madder and madder...

Then she turns around quickly, giving me no time to move, and walks straight through me.

Electricity fires through my body and hers and she leaps away, closer to the back door. Everything in me is on edge. I didn't know it would feel like that. I've only been brushing my hand against her lately. I hadn't tried to move through her, and this was a moment of pure luck. I feel alive. Something deep inside me pulses, and I want to do it again.

She glances back and her eyes are filled with fear. A shudder ripples through her and she pulls her coat tighter. Colour drains from her face, making her look deathly pale. In fact, I could swear she's about to vomit. Instead, she scrambles with *the back door. There's a tiny whimper that escapes her. Once inside, she slams the door and rapidly locks it behind her.*

Standing alone in the garden, I take in the night air for a moment. She thinks she's locked me out here with the screeching owls and screaming foxes. I take a look at the ancient bath beneath the great tree. What a waste.

Rage is now replaced with satisfaction and a new sense of adventure. I step through the back door with ease.

Chapter Eighteen

Flora

I didn't go to sleep until nearly two am that night. Charlie and I spent all night messaging one another, and I was far too excited to sleep anyway. Mum had tried to get all the gossip, but I had made a cheeky remark stating that if she wrote three chapters, I'd tell her every gory detail. This fell a lot flatter than I'd expected, and she'd just filled her wine glass and disappeared into the dining room. Suited me fine though.

I didn't tell her about the thing in the garden. It felt like the wind had electrocuted me, or it was something to do with this stupid thing on my arm. Maybe I was starting to hallucinate. Jesus, what if I was starting to go mad?

I couldn't be having that now that I had a cute boy and a best friend to be worrying about. I spent the rest of the night texting them both: Charlie sending me sweet things and Lydia and I swapping news on our love lives.

I must have fallen asleep while messaging at some point though, and I was quickly assaulted with horrible dreams. I woke after barely an hour of sleep and checked my phone. There was a message from Charlie with a GIF of a sleeping Disney princess. Rubbing the sleep from my eyes, I plugged my phone in to charge and then lay back down, snuggling into the duvet.

As I tried to drift off, I felt something heavy press down on the mattress next to me. Eyes opened to reveal nothing. Then something touched my arm. It was cold and it lingered, sliding up my upper arm and tracing my shoulder. Something tendril-like slid over my pyjama top and found my collar-bone. I imagined it was fingertips. I scrambled up into a sitting position and tried to push the unseen hands away, but another invisible hand materialised to touch my cheek. Again, I tried to push it back.

"No," I said, loud and firmly. "No."

Worse was yet to come as something cold pressed against my lips.

I had no way to pull away as I had my head pressed against the headboard from my first attempt to back off. Waving my hands in front of my face, whatever it was seemed to dissipate.

"I said no!" I repeated. In my panic, I thought I heard something snicker.

Staring into the dark, I saw nothing. I strained my eyes against the night, desperately searching for an explanation. Nothing.

Gathering up my duvet and pillow, I decided to sleep on the couch downstairs. Then after twenty minutes of trying to get comfortable, I realised that I'd left my phone upstairs.

Bugger.

For a brief moment, I decided I could live without it. I didn't need to be checking it every two minutes. But then I thought about Charlie and Lydia, and I realised that it would be like chopping off my arm.

I decided to go upstairs, grab it, and then make a beeline back down to the couch.

As I stepped into my room, my PC monitor lit up. Spotify was on the screen, and it had up a playlist I'd never seen before. It was called "For Flora." The speakers crackled and a song I'd never listened to before started to play—"New Modern Love" by Halestorm. The shriek of a guitar gave me a fright, and I scrambled to turn it off. Mum was in bed, and I wasn't waking her up with some angry female-fronted rock band. I turned off the computer and pulled the plug out of the wall.

I took in the darkness of the room. In the corner, something watched me.

"I don't want you in here, Miles," I said defiantly, trying make it clear that I wouldn't put up with this. "This isn't your room anymore."

We were in a silent stand-off. I was sure I could feel breath against my face. I stood my ground until it stopped.

I grabbed my phone and left the room, closing the door behind me and wishing I could lock him away that easily.

❧

When I finally drifted off on the couch, I dreamt that I found myself in a world of fire and rust and iron. Shades of amber surrounded me as I walked through a horrible version of my house that was made of old rusted metal. Something beckoned in the world outside and I foolishly obeyed its call. Pushing the heavy front door open with a hideous scraping noise, I was confronted by a world of flames.

Out on the island out in the water, a bright orange beacon burned. It stood like an angry lighthouse and pulled me closer. At the edge of the pond, I looked down, not knowing how I'd cross. As I stepped on the water, the heat from my feet burned the ground like a brand and the water crept away from me, hissing with steam as it evaporated around me. I crossed with an ease that made me uncomfortable. When I reached land, the water closed up behind me, trapping me on the overgrown island.

"Hello, lover," a deep voice rang out behind me. I turned around to find the man himself: Miles Allen.

He stood in the middle of the island wearing nothing but a pair of low-hung black skinny jeans. His left arm hung at his side, torn and useless. His dark hair draped over his face, acting as curtains for those penetrating green eyes. His skin was so pale it was practically translucent.

Frankly, I found his lack of a shirt a little ridiculous.

Maybe it was because this was a dream. Maybe it was because I was buoyed up after a successful date. Or maybe I was just so sick of his nonsense. I suddenly found myself filled with the levels of irritation I felt when Phil had tried to confront me in the canteen. This boy had picked the wrong night to try to talk me over.

"I knew you'd find me eventually," he said in that almost put-on dramatic deep voice. "We were always going to find each other." His eyes were lined with smudged black paint, making him look like a sort of sinister Robert Patinson with none of the charm.

"Erm, no," I told him, stifling a laugh. "I'm here to ask you to stop ruining my things, leaving stains on my bed, and touching me when I've already told you not to."

"You're the one who's been hanging around my bedroom," he said with a smirk. "You came back after I touched you."

"I wasn't coming back to you, I was getting my phone! It's not your room anymore; it's mine," I told him. "And even if it was, being in your bedroom is not an invitation."

He stepped forward, and I could smell damp. That smell when you've left a towel on the bathroom floor for just a little too long. His left hand twitched, as if the tendons and muscles were trying to order it to move, but it kept shorting out, like a lamp trying to light when the wires were frayed.

"You're in my house, little girl. My house: my rules."

He smelled worse the closer he got. My eyes stung.

"You're going to stop this nonsense and come over here to stay with me," he ordered. With a wave of his right arm, he gestured to the world on fire around him.

"I don't want to stay here," I told him. The smell was starting to cloud my head, choking my throat and holding my words back. "Nobody would."

Only a minute ago, I was filled with angry rage and determined to put him in his place. Now, he loomed over me. Smoke swirled around him, occasionally knocking his bangs away from those eyes. Something inside warned me to run. I can't. I wanted to, but now that we were this close, I was afraid. I was more afraid of him than I had ever been.

Stephanie lingered in my mind.

I thought about every time I've read about women who stay with abusive men. I thought about how I felt when Stephanie talked about staying with Miles. And now I understood why. This fear. This fear that shut me up and drilled my feet to the floor. This was what kept her with him for so long. That horrible feeling of "what is he going to do next?"

Again, there was a spasm in the fingers of his left hand.

I flinched, assuming he was going to hit me. The corner of his mouth crept upwards, and he looked proud of himself. I hated myself for letting him see how scared I was.

"You saw that bitch Stephanie," he growled. "Did she tell you what I was capable of? Did she tell you more lies?"

"She told me that you were trying to make her do things she didn't want to."

"Liar. She told me she'd die for me. Then when push came to shove, it was her doing the shoving." Part of me could imagine teen goth Stephanie saying things like *"I'd die for you"*, but always in a melodramatic way. She never actually meant that she wanted to die at seventeen for eternal love.

"She also told me that she didn't want you to die either."

"More lies," he said. The fire around us seemed to be climbing higher. I couldn't see the edges of the island anymore. He had me trapped here. "See for yourself."

His right arm shot up, and he placed a hand over my eyes. The shock of it rocked me backwards, but somehow, he'd got me, and I didn't fall. Instead, a red flare flashed before me, and I wasn't on the island anymore. I was standing in the bathroom of my house but not as it is now. This picture didn't quite seem right. It looked like a piece of paper that had been dropped in a puddle. The edges rippled and every now and then colours would bloom before me.

There was a slow dripping sound. The cold tap dripped into an already full bath. Miles lay in it, brandishing a kitchen knife. His left arm was already bleeding, and his breathing struggled. Red trails danced over the surface of the water. He wasn't naked but shirtless and wearing low rise jeans. Behind me, there was something that sounded like a distorted scream and Stephanie ran past me as if I wasn't there.

Words were tangled in this watery hell, and I couldn't make out what anyone was saying. All I could do was watch as Stephanie tried to pull Miles out of the bath. With a monsoon of bathwater, they both eventually wound up on the floor. Stephanie was crying and trying to wrap a towel around his arm. Clothes were soaked through with bloody water. None of her words came out whole but she looked like she was trying to help. Miles was drifting in and out of consciousness.

With the last of his strength and his one good arm, he pulled the knife, and it was clear—even without understanding his words—that he was threatening her. She was frantically shaking her head but still trying to save him. The knife searched pitifully for her throat, but she easily knocked it away. Her tears were a waterfall as she kept shaking her head. More garbled words came, and Miles said something through gritted teeth. I'd never seen more hate in a person's face.

Next, a faceless parent walked in and instantly started making inhuman wails. The woman had no face, just a black void where her face should be. I could only assume this was Miles' mother. She pressed herself against the bathroom wall and her hand landed where her mouth used to be. The mother-thing made more horrible noises. She pointed wildly at Stephanie who continued to cry.

With his last breath, Miles spat on Stephanie.

Bathwater continued to overflow until it was around my ankles. It swept up Miles and Stephanie, and the mother-thing didn't seem to notice. The water levels kept rising until I started to panic.

"This is bullshit, Miles!" I screamed. "Let me out. This is nothing Stephanie didn't tell me." The water was at my knees now. "And not letting me hear what everyone is saying is a joke. How can you think that you're giving me a clearer picture with this?"

Water lapped my thighs as the mother-thing kept screaming.

"I think you're the liar. I think Stephanie did everything she could to save you. And now you're stuck here and she's getting on with her life."

My waist was wet now, and I was having to hold my bad arm over the putrid water. The smell was awful. It was damp, death, and decay all in one breath.

"I'm not your replacement for Stephanie. She did the right thing, and I'm not here to fill that void in your life. I'm not getting dragged under with you."

From under the murky water, the corpse of Miles rose up and his right hand grabbed me by the throat. "Poor choice of words," he growled and, this time, every syllable was crystal clear.

He plunged me under, and my mouth and nostrils filled with dirty water. Eyes wide and nails clawing at his arm, I fought and fought and fought.

Then the blackness started creeping in...

Chapter Nineteen

Flora

I woke violently to discover that the person touching me was not my undead assailant, but my mother. She looked more afraid than I'd ever seen her, and she was yelling at me to wake up. Confusion painted my face as a wave of cold sweat swept over me. Thoroughly disorientated, I managed to mumble "Mum" and grab her wrist.

"Oh, thank God, Flora," she gushed. Tears wet her cheeks and snot hung from her nostrils. "Flora, sweetie, what are you playing at? You've been yelling on the bathroom floor for the last twenty minutes."

The bathroom? Sure enough, I was sitting on the bathroom floor, wedged between the end of the bath and the wall.

"Yelling?" I asked.

"Mostly *I'm not getting dragged under by you*," Mum informed me. "Come on, let's get you out of there."

Taking my hand, Mum pulled me out of the cramped corner I'd squashed myself into. The sudden movement did not agree with me. Quickly, I let go of her and scrambled to the toilet bowl on my hands and knees. Nausea crashed into me as I heaved. It felt like I was spewing up the contents of a rusty old kettle. More water than I ever could have drunk came spilling out of me. A sickening taste of iron filled my mouth.

The vomit went on for what felt like longer than it probably was. At my side, Mum held my hair back the whole time. When it eventually stopped, I sat back, falling onto my butt like a toddler, tired from learning to walk. I realised that my pyjamas were wet and clinging to my skin.

Obviously noticing my confusion, my mum tried to explain. "When I came in, the tap was running. I think you might have tried to have a bath."

Throwing the offending claw-footed bath some vicious side-eye, something shiny caught my attention. With my remaining strength, I reached out and grabbed the object. It was a knife. A very big kitchen knife. The handle was clean and looked brand new. However, the blade was dirty and stained brown and orange with what I hoped was rust.

Beside me, Mum gasped. "That's one of our knives. It's been missing for days. Why does it look like it's been there for months? We haven't even been here for months..." This was her nervous chatter, and it was exactly where I got it from. "And it's supposed to be stainless steel! This is the exact opposite of stainless; this is *stained* steel!"

I scrunched up my face and handed her the phantom object. "And you're supposed to be the writer in the family." I tried to get to my feet. Making my way to the sink, I was horrified by my reflection as it stared at me from the mirror.

My eyes were heavy and sunken. My skin was sweaty, greasy and almost translucent. I looked as though I was dying.

"Jeez," I muttered, reaching up to prod at my limp cheek.

"Flora!" Mum exclaimed. "Your arm!"

Turning my arm over, I discovered that the wound on my forearm looked positively alive. Dark red edges of the gash gave way to purple veins that pulsated, pushing their venom throughout my body. Just looking at it made my head throb.

"Shit," I mumbled, leaning on the sink for support.

Behind me, Mum was attempting to snap into action, but I could see the panic in her face. I watched her in the mirror as I tried to splash myself awake with cold water.

"Right, I'm phoning a doctor. No, I'm phoning an ambulance..."

"Mum..."

"...this is a very nasty infection, and it needs..."

"It needs rest. We can see a doctor in the morning..."

"Oh, we are not waiting..."

"Yes, we are..."

"...you've been sick, and you're apparently delirious if you've been sleepwalking..."

While Mum babbled, the whispering that had been following me for weeks started to claw its way back into my ears, burrowing into my brain and grasping at anything it could get a hold of. It yanked control of the wheel, steering me straight towards saying something hateful. My face hurt and I watched in the mirror as my features warped and became something otherworldly. This couldn't be happening.

I fought and fought and fought.

"She says she doesn't want to leave this house, you bitch," bellowed the voice that had hijacked my mouth.

In my head, I yelled a silent 'No' and reclaimed my body.

Mum's face was filled with horror. Her hand clasped over her mouth. I spun around, away from the sink, and wrapped my arms around her.

"That wasn't me," I whispered frantically in her ear. "I promise that wasn't me. I know I've been an idiot before but, I swear, I didn't say that."

She took a little moment before she hugged me back. That delay—the wait to see if she'd hold me and trust me again—hurt more than my arm did.

"Come here," Mum eventually said, folding her arms around me. We held each other for a long time. Probably more than we actually needed to. But we were both shaking. Whether that was from fear or my cold, wet pyjamas, I still don't know.

"Mum, there's something in this house," I hissed. Tears crept from my eyes. "And I think it wants to hurt me."

Unpeeling herself from our hug, Mum looked me in the eye. For a minute or two, she said nothing, just wiped my tears away.

I could see her wrestling with her common sense. There was no way that a supernatural creature could be trying to kill her daughter, but tonight's bathroom incident was far too difficult for her to explain.

She exhaled deeply. "Go change into clean pyjamas, and I'll tidy up in here," she said. Her panicked voice had drained away and the mum voice was back; the kind that acted like she was dealing with bed-wetting rather than a brief tangle with possession. "Then we're going downstairs for a cuppa, and we're going to talk this whole thing through."

I nodded and she steered me into my room before she vanished back into the bathroom. Like a dutiful daughter, I did as I was told but I didn't want to do it in here. I grabbed fresh pyjamas and retreated to Mum's room. Tearing off my damp clothes, I looked at my body in Mum's full-length mirror, which hung on the inside of her wardrobe door.

On my left hip, there was a dark purple bruise that was unmistakably in the shape of a hand. Shaking, I measured it against my own palm. It didn't match. I covered it up quickly and made my way downstairs. Two cups of tea were hastily made as I tried to ignore the sounds of Mum crying in the bathroom.

We retired to Mum's library and, over steaming hot tea, I told her everything.

By the time I was finished, it was after three am. Mum didn't ever interrupt me. Only asked the occasional question. She wrote everything down, dating each event. The ones she had been present for were the ones she nodded her head through. This seemed to be clearing some things up for her.

Finally, she closed the notebook and looked over at me. She sighed for about the millionth time that night.

"I'm sorry," I whispered.

"Oh, sweetie, what have you got to be sorry for?" she asked with a comforting smile.

"We're going to have to move," I sniffled. "That's the only way the last girl got rid of him."

Mum shook her head firmly. "Nope. We've already had to move because of a living man. We're not moving for a dead one."

The absurdity of this statement struck me, and I laughed. Mum did too.

"I love you, Mum."

"Love you too, sweetheart."

Him

I didn't know I could do half of that. I'm exhausted but I feel exhilarated too. I think I'm getting more powerful. The more scared she is, the mightier I feel.

The rush when I was holding her under the water felt unbelievable. Better than anything I ever felt when I was alive. Better than music, better than sex, better than thinking Stephanie loved me.

Emma Kathryn

I wasn't going to kill her. Not then. Actually, I wasn't sure if I physically could kill her. There was nothing to actually drown her, but she was gasping like she couldn't breathe. I imagined my heart beating faster (even if it's not there anymore) as I watched her struggle and felt her grab at me. It was amazing.

I wasn't going to kill her.

But if I was, she'd be here with me forever. And then she'd really understand that she has no choice other than to love me.

I should have tried this when Stephanie was still around.

Flora thinks I was showing her lies about Stephanie. Says I was only showing her my side of the story because I didn't let her hear all the words. But the truth is, I don't remember. I don't remember everything Stephanie said while I was lying on that bathroom floor, watching all my regrets bleed out of me. I wish I could. I've had fifteen years of reliving that night over and over again in my head, but I still don't know what words she said to try to get me out of that bathtub.

I really wish I knew.

All I remember is the feelings. Being angry and scared and wondering what the hell I'd just done.

Chapter Twenty

Flora

Sunday morning felt like a million miles away from drinking tea in the dining room. I woke on the couch, head buried under an old knitted blanket, feeling a weight on my legs.

"Missus, you sleep like the dead," a voice crooned over me. Painted nails dragged the blanket away from my face. Lydia loomed over me, pinning my legs down with her butt.

"What do you expect with a big goth tombstone pushing me down?" I groaned. "What are you even doing here?"

"Your mum called us first thing."

"Who's us?"

"The Ghostbusters."

"Shut it," I grumbled, before pushing her off me and crashing her to the floor. She landed with a thud and made a noise as if all the air had been pushed out of her.

"Damn you," she heaved and yanked me onto the floor with her.

We laughed until I twisted a funny way and pain shot up my left arm. My laughter instantly stopped and was replaced by an anguished hiss. Lydia and I untangled, and she took my wrist, turning my arm so that she could see the damage. It was hidden under bandages though.

"Seriously, that's not right."

I gently pulled my arm back. "You think I don't know that?" I asked, cradling my limp arm against my body. Hot, searing venom pushed its way upwards. It was quickly replaced with a cold sweat. This felt a lot like dying. I grumbled and got to my feet. She helped me steady myself and looked me up and down.

"Anyway, it's just you and me, kid. Everyone else is busy. And you look like shit, so just as well I'm the only one exposed to the horror."

"Gee, thanks."

"That's a professional opinion, FYI. Lisa's mum is the local doc, and she was here when you were all feverish and still sleeping. She just said, *she looks like shit; that's my professional opinion.*"

I wracked my brain. Had I really seen a doctor that morning? Lydia suddenly looked a little worried.

"She said you had an infection and prescribed fluids and antibiotics," she quickly informed me.

"I don't remember seeing a doctor," I whispered.

"That's okay," Lydia told me. Hair fell over my face, and she pushed it away from my eyes.

"I don't think we'll have time for the séance idea," I told Lydia. "This weekend seems to have doubled down on the batshit craziness."

"Who needs a séance when the dead boy is already practically yelling in your face? Come on, time to get up," Lydia said. She took my hand and led me out into the hall. Something creaked above us and I stopped at the foot of the stairs.

The Sunday morning light hadn't reached the upper landing yet. Instead, there was a long looming shadow, reaching down the stairs. The heating rattled a pipe somewhere above us, and the house growled.

Lydia gave a quiet whisper of "come on," and she pulled me towards the kitchen. The dark shape slunk backwards as we moved out of sight.

In the kitchen, Mum and Sara stopped what they were doing when I walked in. The room was quiet save for the ticking of the clock on the wall. Three pm. I had slept for nearly twelve hours. Sara sat upright but Mum stayed where she was leaning on the kitchen island. Dark rings draped around her eyelids like the guilt that draped around my neck.

She forced a smile. "Oh hey, honey, how did you sleep?"

"Weird," I said honestly.

"You seemed really tired," Mum said, reading my mind. "After the doctor left, I just let you rest."

My arm felt heavy. Granted, it was now dressed in a giant bandage. "I don't remember the doctor being in."

"You were pretty out of it," Lydia said. "Lisa called me. She was pretty worried after her Mum came home."

A flutter of panic hit my chest. "Charlie?" I asked.

"He doesn't know," Sara chimed in. "We thought it best not to tell him." In that moment, it dawned on me that Sara knew about Charlie and me. Uh oh.

"He's a worrier," Lydia shrugged. The black knitted poncho she wore danced as she moved. Little silver threads hung from the frayed edges. I realised how well wrapped up everyone was. I stood in only my pyjamas. Everyone else was three layers thick. Was it cold in here? It was hard to tell through the fever.

"We're all just glad you're up, sweetie," Mum said and rose to make me a cup of tea.

Lydia and I sat at the kitchen table. Resting my hands on the table and lifting them again revealed clammy handprints, marking my presence in the most disgusting way possible. Hoping no one was looking, I tried to wipe it away as inconspicuously as possible. It was not my most attractive moment but, hell, it didn't really matter by this point.

A cup of tea appeared in front of me, and I muttered thanks. All eyes in the room stared at me—and another pair that I knew wasn't in the kitchen at that point.

Sara looked sympathetically at me, while Lydia's face was plastered with morbid curiosity.

"Everyone knows then?" I asked Mum, not glancing up from my steaming teacup. "That I've got a dead stalker?" She said nothing so I assumed she nodded. I waited for the judgement of the room.

"I believe you, darling," Sara said with a quiver in her voice. "And Lydia and I are here to do everything we can to help."

Lydia slid her black-nailed hand over mine and gripped it tightly. She didn't seem to notice the sweat and when I lifted my head, I realised that her morbid curiosity was actually the kind of determination that only friends on a mission have.

"I had always hoped that there was something after all this," Sara sighed. "That there was a way for my Robert..."

"Mum..." Lydia snapped, cutting Sara off. "This isn't what we're here for."

For the first time in two months, I wasn't the one creating dramatic tension. Mum and I clocked one another, and she gave me a little shake of her head, signalling not to say anything.

"Of course," Sara said. Sniffing away a tear, she flicked her beautiful hair. She looked so much like Lydia right now. I couldn't believe that there was ever a time I hadn't realised that they were mother and daughter. "But we're here. No matter what you need."

"I just don't want to be alone...with *him*..." I whispered. Saying "with him" made me feel stupid, and I instantly regretted letting the words leave my mouth.

The clock on the wall sounded even louder in the silence. Nobody seemed to want to admit that he was real. They all said they believed me, but nobody was willing to say, "*Let's protect you from the dead boy in the house.*" Instead, it felt like they were whispering "*Let's make sure she doesn't go mad and kill herself like the last kid who lived here did.*"

Something creaked above us again and everyone's heads shot up. It sounded like a rusted pipe shrieking followed by five distinct footsteps. Then it just suddenly stopped.

Lydia's chair scraped back as she jumped up. "For real?" she asked me. In her swift movement, she still hadn't let go of my hand. If anything, she was holding tighter now.

"Ladies, meet Miles," I said, waving to the ceiling. "He's a prick."

For the next few hours, our houseguests seemed more determined to create a distraction from the dead boy living in the walls than actually confront it but, by this point, distractions were welcome.

We watched fluff, followed by some ridiculous true crime documentary that had us all yelling "Who would actually let their kid go with that guy?" at the TV. Take-out was ordered and for a little while, the house felt full of life and laughter. It was good.

No. Scratch that. It was great.

I felt better than I had in the last eighteen hours, and it actually felt like the swelling in my arm was going down. At one point, Mum got up to refill the wine glasses for her and Sara and she touched my forehead.

"Doc seems to have worked wonders on you, sweetie," she said, giving me a proper once over like I was a cat at the vet. "Your colour's coming back and everything."

She disappeared into the kitchen and Lydia looked me up and down. "It's probably me," she said smugly. "My good vibes are healing your soul."

A grin spread against my face. "Totally you. Nothing to do with science."

"To hell with science, lemme cleanse your aura." She laughed and started swiping at the air above my head.

I squealed and tried to push her off.

"Lydia!" Sara reprimanded, but with very little conviction. "You're supposed to be looking after Flora, not getting her all fired up."

We both stopped and looked over at Sara. "Mama, I'm not even going to start on how wrong that sounds," Lydia laughed.

"Oh, stop twisting things, Lydia. Not everything has to be filthy."

Mum appeared with wine and distracted Sara enough to let Lydia and I get back to messing about. The documentary had finished, and there was a sitcom on for background noise. It was pushing 7:00pm now, and the sky was pitch black outside. At some point, Mum had lit the fire in the hearth; this was still a novelty she was getting a bit of a kick out of, and she would find any excuse to light it.

Guilt clung to the bottom of my stomach. Lydia had said it was fine about me seeing Charlie, but I still couldn't shake that I was breaking some kind of rule. This was made all the worse by the whole twin thing.

"About me kissing Charlie," I said, low enough for Sara not to hear.

Lydia sighed and rolled onto her side, so she was facing me and not the TV. "I told you it's fine. Plus, Charlie is super smitten. Can't get in the way of that or he'll kill me."

I didn't know what was a bigger relief, that Charlie had spoken to her about it or that the twin thing didn't exist.

"What did he say?"

"Uh... *I made out with Flora a bit. That cool?* And that was it."

"Oh," I said, feeling like all the air had been let out of me. "*Was* that it?"

Lydia laughed. "Of course not. He wouldn't shut up about you all night."

My chest puffed back up and I felt even better. "Seriously?"

"Yeah, he's got it bad." Blood flooded my cheeks and I tried to fight a smile. "He's away with his skate group today. It was better not to tell him that you were dying and stuff."

"What skate group?"

"He's got a group in the city he skateboards with. They're literally the only friends he has. I know I drag him around stuff at school, but skating is his only normal thing."

Lydia grabbed her phone and started tapping away. After a minute, she swung it round to show me a TikTok video of a bunch of lads skateboarding. Every now and then, Charlie took up the centre of the screen, grinding and jumping and sliding by in a way that was incredibly cool. On one occasion, he and another boy pouted at the camera, each flicking their floppy hair out of their eyes at the same time like they were in a faux make-up tutorial. The other boy had a pierced lip and tattoos. Charlie looked the youngest in the group by a good year or so. He looked so happy. A million miles from the boy who helped his mum with dance classes and got picked on at school.

Watching this made me like him even more.

"Aye, alright," Lydia said, pulling her phone away. "That's enough for you, pervert."

I giggled an apology and realised that we had run out of juice. Lydia offered to get up, and she disappeared into the kitchen.

Mum and Sara continued to chatter away about their lives beyond Scotland. They were comparing the cities Sara had been to for dance competitions and where she'd grown up in Spain with the places Mum had been to on book tours. It was nice to see Mum smiling and animated again. She needed this. She needed a companion. Spending weekend evenings with her teenage daughter wasn't enough. This is the kind of friend we both needed.

A wild wind swept through the living room out of nowhere. It silenced Mum and Sara and blew the fire in the hearth out. A plume of smoke danced around the centre of the room, pirouetting away from the blackened logs. Everyone sat upright.

"Where is Lydia?" Sara said in a panic. An answer came quickly enough as a glass crashed in the kitchen. The mothers scrambled to their feet, and I got up as quickly as my fuzzy head would let me.

In the kitchen, Lydia stood frozen, staring at the window above the sink. It was covered with foggy condensation, as if the hot tap had been running for too long. Letters were slowly appearing in the condensation, forming words then sentences and then being wiped clear by some invisible hand, only to start all over once the condensation had reformed.

"What does it say?" I asked, touching Lydia's shoulder and making her jump. Her concentration shifted mostly away from the window to me, but she kept glancing back.

"Never loved you anyway...ran off with her...drunk drunk drunk..."

Behind us, Sara let out a little sob. I took Lydia's hand again. "It's not him," I told her. My words were true. I knew exactly who it was. I had seen that handwriting often enough.

"How do you know it's not?" Lydia choked on the question. Each word was a struggle for her. The letters were still forming. The last ones I saw before deciding I didn't want to see any more were "stupid brother too..."

"For a start, what would your dad be doing in this house?" I said, hitting her with the coldest truth first to wake her up. It seemed to work but Sara was slipping now.

Behind us, Mum was whispering something to Sara, trying to calm her down. It wasn't exactly working.

"...But it might be..."

"Mum," Lydia snapped. "Dad didn't give enough of a shit about us when he was alive, why would he be bothering now?"

"You don't mean that," Sara argued back. "He loved all of us."

"He was drunk with some woman he'd met at a dance competition and crashed his car. There was no way he was thinking of us then, was he?"

Somewhere deep within me, I felt a dark laugh rise up. Miles was trying to push me down again. I fought him and fought him hard, leaning on the kitchen table and letting the fighting around me drift away. Far away. A pulse throbbed in my arm, threatening my improving health. Shaking my head, I tried to fight him.

He was enjoying this, I knew it.

Something in the house banged, and I returned to the world of the living once more. The kitchen was empty. I'd blacked out again.

Voices rang out in the garden. I wiped away the filth and condensation from the window, revealing Mum and Sara outside. When did they go out? Sara was weeping and Mum was rubbing her arms.

Stepping back, I went into the hallway. I could hear someone upstairs and prayed that I was hurrying upwards to find Lydia and not Miles. Whispers clawed at my ears as I took the stairs two at a time.

Thankfully, Lydia was draped across my bed, crying just as hard as her mother. The smoky smell from the recently extinguished fire in the living room had found its way up here. It clung to my throat and cloyed at my nostrils. In fact, the entire room looked a little cloudy.

I sat on the edge of the bed and put my hand on Lydia's shoulder.

"He does this," I told her. "Just FYI, I was screaming at my mum last night because she suggested I go to the doctor. He doesn't seem to like conversations that don't involve at least a bit of yelling. He also seems to have mother issues..."

"It's true though," Lydia mumbled into the duvet. For a brief moment, I dreaded to think how much mascara and eyeliner she had streaked over my bedsheets. Not that that mattered right now.

"After we were born, Mum tried to get back into dancing. She really did. But she was exhausted. When she decided to back off a bit, Dad was barely ever home. He was always chasing glory, and girls *looooved* him. I know he didn't want us. We were a burden. Us and Mum." Lydia sat up and tried to wipe her face with the back of her hand. "She doesn't ever see it that way though. She practically worshipped him and just kept acting like everything was fine any time he'd come home. I mean, she moved across Europe for him. They settled here because it was close to my grandparents on Dad's side. Not that Dad gave a shit about them either. But Mum did. She thinks they're great. Plus, she was so convinced Dad was going through some kind of crisis. That it would be just a phase. And when he died, it was the end of the world."

My mind went back to the framed pictures all over the house and even Charlie's attitude towards talking about his father.

"I really thought she was getting better when she opened that bloody dance studio. Part of me thinks Charlie did too and that's why he's there all the damn time. Obviously, it's done nothing," Lydia cried.

"No," I said, filling with anger and rage. "This is *his* fault. It's Miles..."

The whispering got louder, and I waved my hand in the air, trying to shake off whatever was leaning close to my ear.

Words were forming and they were no longer incoherent whispers. *You've gone and frightened the weird girl off,* he laughed. It was the same voice as the boy I met in my dream. It was Miles.

I saw worry spread across Lydia's face. She took my wrists and lowered my hands from my ears. Lips moved but I couldn't hear anything she was saying. Instead, the only words I heard were from him.

Tell her to bugger off...get rid of her...get her out NOW...

"Why don't you bugger off instead?!" I yelled into the air.

An expression of pain flickered across Lydia's face as the world came rushing back with a loud pop of my ears.

"Not you." I started to beg, pulling her in for a hug. "Bloody hell, not you, please."

We hugged and fell to our knees on the floor. I don't know which one of us was crying. Maybe both.

Around us, everything creaked, and the walls seemed to lean. Lydia gasped and jumped back away from me. The house was so loud.

My speakers burst to life and started playing music from his playlist again. This time, my phone informed me it was a song called "Scarlet" by In This Moment.

He was getting stronger. Last night Miles had crossed some invisible line, and now, he could do whatever he wanted.

Well, not anymore.

"Right," I said, suddenly filled with determination. "We're getting rid of this bastard."

It was different when it was just me that he was giving a hard time. But over the last twenty-four hours, he'd gone for my mum, my best friend, and even my best friend's mum. It was time to be done with him.

On the bed, Lydia's phone started to vibrate. On the screen appeared the word "*Mama*."

"That's weird," Lydia said, answering the call and putting it onto speaker.

"Lydia, honey, let us back in the house," her mum yelled over a storm on the other end of the phone. "We need to—"

Voices gave way to crackling static and Lydia dropped her phone as if it had just electrocuted her.

Interference shrieked through the iPhone, followed by a metallic voice that sounded like an old voicemail.

You're going to die in here. You should have listened to your dumb cow of a mother. Leave the girl alone, she's mine. She's mine. She's mine. Stupid dumb cow of a mother. She'll die out there. You'll kill her like you killed your waste of a father...She's mine. The girl is mine. The girl...

I snatched the phone and hung up.

"He's locked us in," I said, trying not to let the fear in my voice out.

Sheer horror filled Lydia's tear-rimmed eyes. She was still staring at the phone.

"Lydia," I said trying to pull her back into the world of the living. I grabbed my keys from my bedside table. "I need you to go try to let them back in." I pressed the keys into her hand and hoped the cold metal would ground her. "I know what to do. But I need to be able to get outside. So, you've gotta unlock the back door and check that both our mums are safe, okay?"

A frantic nod shook its way out of Lydia's head. Fingers tightened around the keys.

"What are you going to do?" she asked.

"Something really stupid."

Lydia ran down the stairs, clinging to the banister the whole way. Somewhere in the house, something crashed, and Lydia screamed.

"I'm okay, I'm okay," quickly rang out from downstairs, and I realised that the crashing noise was coming from Mum's library.

Now was not the time to check it though. While Lydia was downstairs, I went into the hall and pulled the attic door open. A ladder swung down to meet me.

I knew what I'd find up there.

The cardboard box of crap would be up there.

Stephanie's words came back to me. All the nonsense stopped when she burned his stuff. She'd passed it off as a joke, but that was it. I needed to burn the stuff he kept bringing back into the house. The yearbook, the jacket, the aftershave, the notepads...

Everything.

Emma Kathryn

It had to burn.

Scaling the ladder, I pushed my head into the attic. The light was on because it always was these days. There was never any point in turning it off because he'd just turn it back on. I was sick of the sound of the light string being pulled in the middle of the night.

Shadows skirted around the rafters, reaching out from the points where the roof met the walls. Dark hands were desperate for me, but I didn't want them. I cursed myself for the early nights when I tricked myself into reading his journals and looking for deeper meaning in them. This wasn't a dark mysterious figure to tame and care for. This was a cancer to cut out and be done with.

Sure enough, the box sat in the centre of the room. I grabbed it without a worry for what he'd do to me. Nor was I particularly careful with its contents. To hell with that.

In the corner of my eye, I was sure I could see him. A figure stood just outside where the bare bulb's light reached. I did my best to pretend I couldn't see him, but both of us knew fine well that I could. My arm burned as if he was grabbing it tightly and squeezing. The figure stayed where it was. He was messing with my head.

Standing over the trap door, I simply dropped the box to the second floor. Something in the attic screeched. Clasping my hands over my ears, I tried to keep my balance above the ladder. The shriek seemed to travel around the house.

"What the fuck is that?!" Lydia yelled as she fought with the front door.

A laugh gurgled up from my throat. It was finally my own laugh. Not his. He was pissed. This was it—this was what I had to do.

With as much speed as I could garner, I descended the ladder.

About three rungs from the bottom though, there was a sharp yank on my right leg, and I came tumbling to the floor. As my back slammed into the floor, all the air rushed out of my lungs, winding me and leaving me lying next to the devil's box of tricks. My arm throbbed again, reminding me that I was already injured enough.

Pushing myself up, I surveyed the hallway. He wasn't here.

I could see my open bedroom door from here. Nothing.

The bathroom door was also open.

There he was.

His slender figure stood in the bathtub, the shower curtain obscuring his right side, bringing even more attention to his dead left arm. His face was a dark shadow with holes for eyes. Rust ran from the corner of his mouth, dripping slowly from his chin. Those same skin-tight black jeans clung to his jagged hips and his chest was bare. The hems of the jeans were torn and frayed, and their colour had run as if left outside on a washing line and forgotten about for months on end.

His mouth opened, dripping more dark orange fluid and the shriek began again.

Spurred on by a mixture of fear and determination (probably about a seventy-thirty split, but I tried hard to convince myself it was the other way around), I gathered up the box. It touched where my arm was bandaged, and I hissed in pain. *Suck it up, Flora,* I told myself and shifted its weight away from the bad part of my arm.

Miles took one step out of the bath. That was enough to make me bolt, and I flew down the stairs. Lydia was still fighting with the door, and I stopped to help.

"Take this," I said, preparing to hand her the box. Quickly, I changed my mind as she reached out to take it. "No no no, wait, don't," I babbled, reconsidering my options. I couldn't let Lydia touch this box. I dropped the box to the floor and Miles let out another animal howl from the top of the stairs.

This was the first time Lydia had seen him. She backed up against the wall beside the door. "Holy hell, Flora," she gasped.

I fought with the keys. Mum started banging on the other side of the door, yelling to be told what was going on. The noise was stabbing at my ears and punching at my head.

With a loud *snickt,* the door finally unlocked. But when I tried to yank it open, it wouldn't budge. I let out an exasperated noise and started pulling on the door.

"Mum, I need you both to push on the other side!" I yelled through the painted glass on the window. We fought and fought, but it wouldn't shift.

Meanwhile, Lydia was still whimpering beside me. I had never seen her like this. That angry, strong, fiery woman was gone, and a little girl trembled under the gaze of the monster in my house. Miles was taking slow steps down the stairs, leaving a trail of amber destruction in his wake.

"Lydia," I snapped, in between pulling on the door. "Lydia, I need you to snap out of it. Yes, there's an undead dickhead on the staircase, but I know how to get rid of him. I need your help."

Still, she didn't move. I slammed my hand against the door in frustration, and it seemed to rouse her. She jumped and looked up at the source of the noise.

"Hey," I said. "You okay? Come on, I need you."

"I'm sorry," Lydia mumbled. Her eyes were bright red, and her hands shook.

"It's fine, it's just..." I looked at the stuck door. "Change of tactic." Addressing mum through the glass window on the door, I yelled, "Round the back. We'll meet you round the back."

I didn't wait for her to answer. Instead, I grabbed the box and urged Lydia to follow. My aim was the kitchen. It involved walking right past Miles but by this point, I just wanted rid of him. Seeing how scared Lydia had been had rattled me. That wasn't how *I* wanted to look whenever I saw him. He was getting high off that fear, and I wasn't giving him the satisfaction anymore.

I walked past the stairs towards the kitchen and Lydia trotted behind me, grabbing onto my shoulder to keep us in constant contact. Smart. If he tried to grab one of us, he'd get both, and we were stronger together.

Once in the kitchen, Lydia threw the door shut and barred it with whatever she could—the bin, a mop and bucket, and a box of recyclables. It wouldn't stop him, but I let her believe that it would. I dropped the box on the island table. The tainted objects called to him and drew him in like a light-house to a lost ship at sea. I had to extinguish that light.

Lydia got to work on the back door which opened with ease. "Why would he lock one door and not the other?" she asked, staring out into the dark of the garden.

"Because he wants me out there," I told her, as I rummaged in a cupboard and found what I was looking for—a box of matches and logs for the hearth in the living room.

Dropping them into the box, I bundled it all up and marched outside. In the kitchen, Lydia's makeshift barricade crumbled with ease. She squealed and followed me out just in time for the kitchen door to burst open.

"What the hell are we doing, Flora?" She wept and grabbed hold of me again.

I grinned, finally sure of myself in a way that I hadn't been since I was back in Glasgow. In fact, surer than I had ever been. I didn't have a damn clue who I was back in Glasgow. I had been a phoney. A queen bee with the theatre kids. A piece of plastic.

Now, I was me.

I was fighting the problems in my life rather than ignoring them.

I was making friends that mattered and who gave a damn about me. Ones I could stand up for and would stand up for me when the time came.

I was Flora freaking James.

"Stephanie said the bullshit stopped with her when she burned all the stuff of his she had," I said, shaking the box triumphantly.

Lydia's face lit up, as if the fire in her belly had reignited. There she was.

"Wanna join me in a bit of a ritual sacrifice?" I asked with an exhausted laugh.

"Always."

Mum and Sara appeared from the side of the house, but I held my hand up for them to stay away. Lydia started to pull things out of the box, and we threw them into the old bath. Even the box itself got chucked in. The stench was unbelievable. Rot came up to meet my nose and it took every inch of strength to fight off puking. Nausea clawed at my stomach, and I felt lightheaded.

"Jesus Christ." Lydia gasped. "This is what I imagine Marilyn Manson smells like."

The shriek came again, and Miles stepped out of the back door. His left arm hung limp, but his right hand was an angry fist. Mum sparked into action and ran at the dead boy. "Stay away from my daughter," she screamed, filled with some kind of terrifying motherly rage.

Miles barely reacted, he just flicked his right hand at Mum, and she flew across the garden, landing in a mess of old dead bushes.

"Mum!" I cried. I wanted to run to her, but I was frozen in place. Sara went to her aid, and I could see that she was okay, just bruised and scratched up. Tears fell down my cheeks as I watched someone else help my mum when I should have been there for her.

And not even only now. I should have been there for her when Dad was being an ass and when she was trying to build a new life for us out of the rubble he'd left behind. I'd been a bitch to her, and she didn't deserve it.

I'd spent my life trying to impress the wrong people. The idiot friends I had back in Glasgow, Dad, and—even if only briefly—bloody Miles.

Miles turned back to me and the bath full of the remains of his life at Blairness High.

Don't, he said in my head, in a voice no one else could hear. This time, there was a sadness in his voice. *I don't want to die again.* I could feel it. But I could also feel his mildew-like tendrils slithering their way into my brain. *I didn't mean it the first time, and I definitely don't want to go now.* I gave myself a shake and Lydia touched my shoulder.

"He's in my head," I whispered. "All the time. He practically lives there now."

He stepped closer. Closer. Closer.

"Then let's evict him," Lydia said. She struck a match and handed it to me.

The closest piece of paper to hand was the note he'd written in my notebook. How that had ever ended up in his box of shit, I'd never know. I let the match kiss it and it curled, reaching for my fingers. I dropped it in the bath and the whole thing lit up like Guy Fawkes' Night.

The old aftershave acted as an accelerant, and the bath was a raging inferno faster than I'd ever expected. Lydia pulled me back and we watched.

A blue fire wrapped around the dead boy standing in the garden. Miles screamed and the ghost face slipped away to reveal his real face, crying and wailing for help. No one else could hear his words. Everyone else heard the noises he and Stephanie had made in my dream. In my head, I could hear it all.

Miles begged for me to save him. *Flora, please. Don't do this. You're killing me.*

"You're already dead," I said aloud as Lydia slipped her hand in mine.

Miles sparked and flashed. Ghostly blue flames danced. His eyes widened desperately. The flames rose and ate his figure, his mouth gaping and he tried to say something else. But it was over. He had nothing left to say to me. We all watched as he flickered out of existence, blue fire and all.

Mum ran to me and wrapped her arms around me. Sara and Lydia had their own reconciliation, but my eyes were still on the very real fire in the bathtub.

The leather jacket puckered and melted while the papers danced and twisted. CDs cracked and the stench drifted off with the smoke. The yearbook burned, and I breathed a deep sigh of relief as fragments of paper blew away in the chill evening breeze.

Miles Allen was out of our house and out of my head for good.

Him

Chapter Twenty-One

Flora

Lydia and I stepped back and admired our handiwork.

"I still can't believe we've managed to pull this off," I said with smug satisfaction. "It's somehow even better than I expected."

"I can't believe we managed to put wallpaper up ourselves yesterday, so I'm a little underwhelmed by the boring paint bit today." She shrugged. It was immediately followed by a grin, and I flicked paint at her.

Laughter filled my freshly decorated bedroom. Lydia and I were each in old baggy T-shirts and leggings that we didn't mind ruining. I'd pulled my hair up in a high ponytail, wrestling all my mad hair away from my face, while Lydia looked eternally graceful with a printed scarf holding hers back in a very Rosie the Riveter inspired look. How she always looked better than me, even when covered in paint, I just didn't know.

"It looks even better than my Glasgow room." I sighed, looking around.

One wall was purple and silver printed wallpaper. It wasn't quite the flocked stuff I'd had before, but this looked nicer. More subtle. We'd painted the rest of the room a purple that matched the wallpaper. Today had indeed been the boring bit: repainting all the trims—doorway, windowsill, and skirting boards—but it was these little touches that marked it as finished.

Over the last month, I'd been making a determined effort to make the room mine. Mum helped me stain the desk a darker colour and I bought a new desk chair. For the walls, I'd been sourcing new *Archival Cycle* fan art prints and, waiting for the paint to dry, was a silver-framed mirror that Mum and I had found in a second-hand shop. Lydia had also provided more candles than a human being could ever need in a variety of shapes, sizes, colours, scents, and *"cleansing abilities."*

Granted, I thought this house was about as cleansed as could be now.

Mum appeared in the doorway, and I could see her fighting the urge to lean against it. "Ladies, it's looking fabulous in here," she said, looking around. She peered at our handiwork, trying not to point out any spots we'd missed. "And, it would seem that Lydia, you have a visitor."

Mum stepped aside to reveal Lauren, carrying a tray of Starbucks drinks. Lydia started to squeal, and I quickly grabbed the drinks so the pair could hug and kiss and reunite. From the hallway, Mum laughed.

"What are you doing here?!" Lydia burst while trying to kiss her at the same time.

"Passed my driving test!" Lauren smiled.

We all squealed choruses of congratulations.

"I decided my first trip should be to join the paint party," she continued, with her face going red with embarrassment. "Which I now see that you've finished." The girls peeled apart, and we let Lauren admire our amazing work.

"Don't worry," Mum said. "I've got charity shop boxes to sort, and now that there's a car between the three of you, you can actually take them for me!"

"Oh joy," Lauren said sarcastically. "I'm so glad I came now."

Mum rolled her eyes and told us to tell her when we were ready, and she'd help us to the car. While I'd been on my own reclaim-the-house kick, Mum had been on hers. We'd finished unpacking, and she'd realised how much of her old life was left in the stuff she'd brought with us. Bit by bit, she'd been deciding what needed a refresh and what she didn't need at all. And now she'd made it to the books, clearing out research for old novels and stuff she'd bought because Dad was working on adaptations and she'd wanted to show an interest or attempt to help (which he never took, to be honest).

That was something I'd come to realise. Dad never produced original stories. He was always adapting other people's work.

The best thing about Mum's life revamp was that she'd started writing again. A ghost story this time. A little on the nose, if you ask me, but her agent loved it. Especially when she told her about the house (well, an extremely edited version of the story of our house). It wasn't about Miles, nor was it about me, which was a relief. Instead, it was a good old traditional gothic romance. I couldn't be prouder of her.

I picked up the paintbrushes and paint and left Lydia and Lauren alone for a bit. Once I'd dumped it all in the kitchen, I grabbed a seat at the counter and started to send Charlie pictures of the finished room. He was off skating again today —that's what Sundays were for when it came to Charlie, and I liked that we each had our own thing. He could go skate, and I could hang with Lydia.

Things with Charlie had been going well. Slowly and gently, but my stomach was still filled with electricity every time I saw him. Lydia still didn't mind, which I thought was the most important thing. I'd somehow managed to balance having a friend and a boyfriend in the same family without pissing either of them off or stressing me out.

Charlie sent back compliments and then a picture of his day's work: an almighty gash on his knee. The perils of being a skater, apparently. He asked if I wanted to pop round for pizza once he'd gotten home and I'd finished redecorating, and I said I'd love to.

Filled with optimism, I set about washing out the paint-brushes in the big Belfast sink. Hot water filled the deep square-shaped bowl and steam rose up above me, coating the kitchen window with condensation. Absent-mindedly, I wiped it away and looked out.

Nothing appeared at the windows anymore—no faces, no horrible words, no Miles. Beyond that, the broken bathtub was gone. Mum had called the council to get it picked up the day after the cursed bonfire. All that was left was a slight char on the tree it had been sitting under and a stain on the grass (which Mum was already yammering on about getting lifted and replaced once spring came around).

"You okay, sweetie?" Mum said, coming into the kitchen and giving me a fright.

"Yup," I said honestly and turned the tap off. Drying off the brushes on the edge of my t-shirt instead of ruining a tea towel, I drained the cloudy water. "Just giving Lauren and Lydia some time alone. And making sure you have no mess to yell at me for."

"That's my girl!" Mum said and gave my shoulders a squeeze. "I'm proud of you, you know that, right?"

"For washing paintbrushes?" I joked.

"You know what I mean."

"I'm proud of you, too, Mum."

"Shhhh, enough of that," she said in her usual dismissive way when she didn't want to admit she was a trooper.

As she slid her hand down from my shoulder, she turned my arm around, revealing the scar on my left forearm. "Barely noticeable now," Mum lied. It had healed well, but it was a cracker of a scar. A constant reminder of the hold Miles had had, not just over this house, but over me.

"Maybe I could get a tattoo to cover it up?" I suggested. Already, I knew what the answer would be.

"Absolutely not," Mum said. "And for that outrageous idea, you can help me start loading up books."

"It would be a very tasteful one," I continued as I followed her into the dining room, where she had five boxes of charity shop fodder. "Like a naked lady fighting a dragon."

"What happened to the traditional "*I heart Mum*" that all the sailors used to love?" Mum joked and passed me a box.

"Okay, so no tattoo then."

"I'm so glad we finally agree on something."

I shouted at Lydia and Lauren from the bottom landing, and they appeared, holding Lauren's mum's car keys aloft like a mighty trophy. We piled up on boxes and headed out to the car. It was March and the days were starting to get a bit longer. The house was filled with sunlight and, while there was still that early spring chill, it wasn't quite so cold and dreary anymore.

"Guess who's started reading the *Archival Cycle*?" Lydia asked as she waited for Lauren to open the boot.

"Well, I thought I better see what all the fuss is about," Lauren shrugged. We started to slide boxes in the back of the car. "Plus, Lydia never shuts up about it."

"No way!" I beamed and passed her another box. "Do you like it? What do you think? Are you officially an *Archivist* yet?!"

"I can see the appeal," Lauren said reluctantly. "The whole guild system thing is quite cool. I can see how people could get sucked into it. That stupid talking coat is ridiculous though."

Lydia made a face in my direction, and I giggled. "She doesn't know what she's talking about," she groaned. Then, her face lit up like she'd just remembered something. "Oh, did you see they released set photos of the assassin's guild?"

"No," I said. I hadn't been looking for *Archival* show updates. Not for weeks. Part of me was willing to draw the line between the show and the books. The other part genuinely wasn't interested anymore. The books were mine. The guild in my head was never going to be the guild in the show and that was fine.

Lydia whipped her phone out and started scrolling. Lauren hunched round her as I pushed the last box into the car. It had RESEARCH written over it in black Sharpie.

"What do you think?" Lydia asked and thrust a set photo into my face.

There was a lot of green fabric draped in the background—CGI would undoubtedly be doing most of the heavy lifting—but it looked okay, I guess. Silver shields lined the walls, and the deep red carpets did actually match what I'd imagined. Actor Jason Issacs strode through the halls; I'd missed the news that he'd be playing Ophie's father. It was a good fit, actually. The last casting news I'd read was that John Boyega would be the captain of the Guardian's Guild, which I'd been really pleased about. The last picture was the actress playing Ophie (whose name I'd already forgotten) standing under the great stone raven in the courtyard of the Guild. There was something not quite right about its face. That was annoying.

Lydia snatched her phone away. "The raven's a disaster," she sighed. I wouldn't quite have gone that far, but I knew she was doing it for my benefit. She'd worked out that if she did all the TV show research, I wouldn't fall down a Google rabbit hole, and I was thankful for that.

We piled into the car and Lydia put the details of the charity shop in town into her phone, putting it into the mount Lauren had on the dashboard for sat-nav use. I piled into the back seat as Lauren flicked through Spotify for something for us to listen to. Once we were all good and Mum waved us off, we set off on the road to the shop. For what was a half-hour walk the rest of the time, the maps app claimed we could drive there in seven minutes. Even if I had finally accepted our move here, I still hated how far away we were from everything.

"You'll never guess who we might see today." Lydia laughed, stretching round to see me from her spot in the front passenger seat. "Pencil dick Phil."

"What?!" I quizzed, straining against my seatbelt.

"Turns out you weren't the only person he'd been giving hell on Twitter, and his mum found his account and freaked out. Made him get a part-time job in the charity shop to learn how to show empathy or some shit like that."

"Brilliant." I laughed.

I leaned back again as Lydia caught Lauren up on the sheer horror that was Phil. Lydia was much better at telling stories than I, and she made our cafeteria showdown sound like a scene from a Western. The Yeah Yeah Yeahs played from the car's tiny speakers. Karen O claimed that "They don't love you like I love you."

My phone began to buzz, and I glanced down to get the biggest shock in months.

Emma Kathryn

DAD CALLING.

A picture of us from a Christmas years ago filled my screen, and my heart beat hard and fast. I looked small in his arms and his smile looked painted on. Lunch churned in my stomach, and I fought the urge to puke out the open car window. My thumb hovered over the green answer button. Then at the last moment, I hit reject.

A huge exhale left my body and Lydia glanced around.

"You okay?" she asked, concern flickering over her face and hiding beneath a smile.

"Yeah," I said as the NEW VOICEMAIL alert flashed up.

I didn't listen to it. Dad could wait around for my call now.

I shoved my phone back into my pocket as we pulled up outside the charity shop. My relaxed smile returned as I realised everything was going to be okay. Mum had been there for everything over the last three months. Dad had no idea of what had happened—in the house, in my new school, or in my life at all.

Mum had. Lydia had. Charlie had.

Hell, even Miles had.

I picked up a box and looked down at my scar. It might have looked awful at one point, but it had healed now. Lydia reached past me and grabbed a box. She gave me a wink.

"Let's go say hi to Phil, shall we?" She grinned and hurried into the Oxfam bookshop on the main street. "Oh hi, Philip! Didn't know you were working. Look out, the feminazis are here, and they brought literature!"

Lauren rolled her eyes as we followed. "Is it wrong that I fancy her rotten when she's like this?" She blushed.

"What, loud and obnoxious?" I said as I propped the door open for her.

"I mean, yeah, but when she's doing it for the people she loves."

Behind the desk in the shop, Phil's face looked like thunder. We dropped five boxes at his feet and Lydia wrapped her arm around Lauren's shoulders. "Have fun, pencil dick," she said with an overdramatic salute and steered Lauren back outside.

I heard her whisper, "Mic drop," and heard Lauren laugh.

I was last to leave. Phil spat, "Hope you're enjoying living in the Murder House."

I stopped in the doorway and shook my head.

"Actually, it's my house now."

THE END

About the Author

Emma Kathryn is a horror fanatic from Glasgow, Scotland. When she's not scaring herself to death, she's either podcasting as one half of the Yearbook Committee Podcast, or she's streaming indie games on Twitch as variety streamer, girlofgotham. Unfortunately, her house is not haunted and she has never seen a ghost.

https://twitter.com/GirlofGotham

https://www.instagram.com/girlofgotham

https://www.twitch.tv/girlofgotham

www.ingramcontent.com/pod-product-compliance
Lightning Source LLC
Chambersburg PA
CBHW061522050726
47503CB00015B/2514